# The People's Friend

## 2021 Annual

# Snap Happy

## by Stefania Hartley

MILY caught a glint of excitement in her mother's eyes when she picked up a little red cardboard envelope from under the Christmas tree.

"This one is for the whole family," Trish trilled, advancing towards her, her whole face alight with expectation.

I guess it's not a new dinner service, then, Emily thought ruefully.

It was also unlikely to be a kitchen utensil, nor any kind of crockery or linen, which would have been welcome.

Perhaps it was one of the pretty miniature cross-stich pictures her mum was so keen on.

But Emily's children had different ideas.

"It's a voucher! I want to open it!" Ethan shot up from the sofa.

"I'm opening it!" Cameron shouted, leaping off the sofa to tackle his brother before he could get to the envelope.

"Your mum will open it," Trish announced, handing the envelope to Emily.

"Then it must be a boring one, like Marks and Spencer's or something," Ethan complained.

"Don't be rude, Ethan," Emily told him. "Whatever it is, you should be thankful."

"Open it, Mum!" Cameron was bouncing up and down on his bottom with the anticipation.

Emily slipped her nail under the red and gold flap, lifted it, then pulled out a ticket.

It was golden, like the ticket that changed Charlie Bucket's life for ever.

*Family portrait voucher. To be redeemed at any of our studios by January 7, 2021.*

Emily felt the smile she had pasted on her face becoming more frozen by the second.

A gift voucher for a family photo! It was very sweet of her mum, and a lovely thought, but not at all suitable for her family.

Family photos were for people with children who could sit still long enough to have their photos taken.

They were for husbands and wives who called each other "Honey" and kissed before they went to work.

*Illustration by Kirk Houston.*

Family portraits were for families where the mum and the dad slept snuggled up to each other, kids cooked breakfast for their parents and the dog never made a mess on the floor.

She and Stuart weren't that kind of couple, and their children were definitely not those kinds of children.

Ethan and Cameron were sure to pull funny faces, stick their fingers out behind each other's heads and poke each other in the ribs when the photographer asked them to look into the camera and tried to hide his growing annoyance.

She and Stuart would stand stiff and tense, as they usually were when around each other, wanting to reprimand the children, yet afraid of creating an atmosphere that was even more awkward.

It wasn't even that they had fallen out: as far as Emily was aware, neither of them had had an affair, spent money behind the other's back or disagreed with the other over the kids' upbringing.

Their relationship had not been afflicted by any of the dramas that had rocked so many other couples' boat.

But they had grown a little weary of each other day by day.

When Stuart's number appeared on her mobile's screen, instead of feeling a little thrill of pleasure, Emily's first thought was, "What's the problem now?"

And she was confident that he thought the same when she called him.

The communication between them was functional and practical – who's picking up the kids from where, who's cooking tonight – and they never wrote or called each other just to say something nice or to ask how the other was.

But that was normal, wasn't it? Honeymoons weren't meant to last for ever.

Emily became aware of the others waiting patiently for the family present to be revealed.

"What is it?" Cameron asked.

Emily freshened up her smile.

"It's a voucher for a family photo! What a kind thought, Mum, thank you!"

As she looked up to smile at her mother, Emily caught the boys rolling their eyes.

Their enthusiasm for the family photo seemed to be no greater than hers.

Well, that voucher would have to disappear in the bottom of a drawer until it was forgotten or expired.

"It's a bit of a selfish present," her mum confessed with disarming candour, "because I'm hoping to get a copy of your family photo. It just struck me that I don't have a nice picture of the four of you. I already have a frame for it."

Oh, no. There was no way Emily could let the voucher expire in the bottom of a drawer if her mum had already bought a frame for the photo and was eagerly awaiting it.

There was nothing else for it. It seemed they would just have to pull themselves together, make the booking, go to the studio and get that photo done.

\*    \*    \*    \*

It didn't start well. The boys refused to put on the shirts and trousers that Emily had put out for them, Stuart complained that the studio was too far, and Emily realised that she had left her lipstick at home only when they were already halfway there.

When they got there, doe-eyed newlyweds and shiny happy families beamed at them from the studio's brightly lit walls.

Just as Emily started comparing her family to the ones on the walls, a man with a curly mop of hair and a broad smile popped up from behind the reception desk and thrust his hand out.

"Hi, I'm Dave and I'm going to be your photographer today. Welcome to the studio."

Emily squeezed out a polite smile. Ethan's hair was sticking out the back like a dodgem antenna, and Cameron must have found the chocolates from last week's party in the car door's pocket, because he had a chocolate moustache.

But before she knew it Dave had rallied them all into a back room with a huge roll-up white backdrop, a forest of dangling silky white umbrellas and black foam shapes.

It looked like the stage of a minimalist theatre. She wondered if Cameron had chocolate on his fingers, too.

Dave closed the door and, with a big cheerful smile and a whirlwind of instructions, started organising them.

"Boys, please, roll that cylinder over here, push the cubes close to it and sit on them – yes, but sideways, good, yes, rest your leg on it: that's great.

"Mum and Dad, perch on the cylinder and turn towards each other."

Emily awkwardly perched on the cylinder with Stuart, both shifting uncomfortably as they battled for space on a surface too small for two bottoms.

"Move closer, that's it – yes, and a little more – perfect!"

Emily found herself pressed against Stuart's side, able to feel the warmth of his body.

"That dangling arm pulls down your shoulder, Dad, and that's not good," Dave pointed out. "Place it round Mum's waist.

"Great job. Smile," Dave went on, but Emily was already smiling. When was the last time that Stuart had held her like that? It felt lovely and familiar.

The camera flashed one, two, three times, and Emily glanced at Stuart. He was smiling, too, at first tentatively, then more confidently.

Whether it was genuine or not, that smile on Stuart's face made her feel warm inside and she realised that she hadn't seen her husband smile for a long time. Too long.

"Boys, one on each side, rest your hands on your parents' shoulders," Dave instructed.

Cameron's little hand gripped Emily's shoulder and she felt the warmth of his childish grip like a delicious tickle. Chocolate fingers? Well, never mind.

The camera flashed again.

"Great job, guys," Dave enthused. "Now I'll count to ten and you'll have to rearrange yourself into a different position, but still touching each other.

"One . . . two . . ."

"Quick, quick!" The boys were getting right into the game as they switched places.

Stuart pulled Emily up on to his knee. She hadn't sat on Stuart's knee for donkey's years.

". . . nine, ten!"

From her husband's lap, Emily beamed to the camera and the boys framed their parents with their arms.

The camera flashed, one, two, three, four times.

"Good job! Again!"

Before changing position, Emily checked Stuart's face. His eyes were sparkling with excitement and he shot her a look of mischievous complicity that made her giggle.

"This is fun!" Cameron shouted, pulling his mum's arm, while Ethan and Stuart rearranged the cubes.

The camera flashed again, and this time Emily found herself leaning against Stuart's chest, their hands clasped together, their free arms around each other's shoulders and waists.

She was so close to him that the scent of his skin made her dizzy with happy memories. Emily felt so happy suddenly that she was almost close to tears.

It was as if Stuart had been away on a very long trip and was now back.

"Great. Now I want to get some shots of the boys on their own," Dave instructed.

Ethan and Cameron enthusiastically replaced Emily and Stuart on the stool and, as they walked away, Emily noticed that Stuart was still holding her hand.

With all her heart she hoped that he wouldn't let go.

The boys posed for the camera then finished with a brotherly hug which moistened Emily's eyes and stretched Stuart's smile.

"Now, let's have Mum and Dad on their own," Dave ordered.

Still clasping each other's hands, Emily and Stuart perched back on the stool.

"How about you look at each other?" Dave suggested.

Before turning to face Stuart, Emily had a moment of trepidation. What if she found that the magic had been broken, that his smile had fizzled away?

Now that she had glimpsed again the spark of loving fun in his eyes, she couldn't bear the thought that the last few camera flashes could break the spell and take everything back to how it had been until just one hour ago.

Tentatively, hopefully, she turned to face her husband. Longing filled his eyes, and she realised immediately from the look on his face that he had missed her, too.

Emily couldn't resist. She leaned forward and pecked his lips with a kiss. Just then, the camera flashed.

"Great shot! We're done!" Dave declared.

\*    \*    \*    \*

After the photo session, Stuart dropped Emily off at home and drove on with the boys to their football training.

The memory of Emily's scent lingered in his mind, as well as the feel of her skin when they had held hands, her twinkling eyes, and that pretty smile . . . He hadn't seen that smile in eons.

For a moment, it had felt like having his old Emily back.

When they arrived at the pitch, the boys waved at him as they skipped to their coach. That was a first: they usually disappeared without so much as a glance.

Stuart felt touched by that and, instead of whipping his phone out of his pocket and checking his work e-mails, he stood at the side of the pitchs and watched them play.

That was a first, too.

## The Birds' Buffet

The morning brought a foot of snow
And birds were huddled in the trees;
Their feeders had quite disappeared
In this unwelcome, sudden freeze.
I had some empty yoghurt pots
And pushed them firmly in the snow
Then put the sun umbrella up
To keep them sheltered down below!
I filled the pots with seeds and grubs
Then watched the quite unusual sight
Of birds crammed on the table top,
So pleased that I had solved their plight!

Eileen Hay.

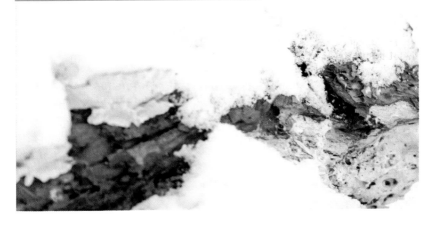

Again, his thoughts drifted back to the photo session. It had been unexpected fun, like they hadn't had in ages.

In the last years, even things that were supposed to be fun, like playing football, had become a serious chore.

He used to love kicking a ball in the garden with his sons before they started proper training. An idea flashed through Stuart's mind and he whipped out his phone.

*Fancy a five-a-side football match next weekend, us and our kids?* he typed to his brothers, and sent it.

Before putting his phone away again, he noticed a message from Emily. Had he forgotten to do something? Had the kids left something at home? He opened it wearily.

*Just to say that I love you. Emily xxx*

Stuart's heart swelled with surprised happiness, and he immediately typed back, *I love you, too xxx.*

Yes, the photo shoot had shone a light in their eyes and left twinkles of possibilities.

On the way home, he stopped by the bakery to buy Emily's favourite cakes, because he had a plan.

As soon as the boys had gone to bed that night, he and Emily would sit in the garden with some wine and a cake to watch the sunset together.

\* \* \* \*

A parcel had arrived in the post.

It was the right shape and Trish was hopeful that this meant the first stage of her plan had been completed.

Still, she had noticed Emily's forced smile when she had thanked her for the voucher at Christmas.

It hadn't taken Jessica Fletcher to work out that Emily had been less than impressed with the gift.

But the fact was that Trish had been worried about Emily and Stuart for a little while now.

She had thought that a family photo, a celebration of their love and what they had created together, would show them what they had and maybe change their perspective a little.

Sometimes she told herself that Emily's marriage was none of her business, but then another part of her mind told her that of course it was.

If Emily had been physically sick, she would have done everything she possibly could to help, wouldn't she?

So if her marriage was sick . . .

Of course, marriages didn't always sparkle. It couldn't always be a honeymoon, and infatuation gave way to satisfied contentment.

But something told her Emily and Stuart seemed to lack contentment, too.

Since handing over the gift at Christmas, Trish had kept telling herself not to get her hopes too high about the photo, because there was a very good chance that Emily would shove the voucher in a drawer and let it "accidentally" expire.

Trish took a deep breath and carried the package into the kitchen.

She delicately cut the brown paper and peeled it away, aware her heart rate had picked up and was thumping with anticipation.

A glossy, happy family was smiling up at her.

Yes, it was Emily's family photo!

As Trish stood up to get the phone to call her daughter, a card fell off her lap on the floor. She picked it up and opened it. It was a thank-you card in Emily's handwriting.

*The family photoshoot was a great success. It was a fantastic idea. Thank you XXXX*

Trish smiled up to her ears. It seemed her little plan had worked after all. ∎

# Cobh, County Cork

The seaport town of Cobh, once known as Queenstown thanks to a visit by Queen Victoria, is steeped in maritime history – not least of all for being *Titanic's* last port of call before disaster claimed so many lives back in 1912. Just three years later the people of Cobh again witnessed a maritime disaster, with the *Lusitania* torpedoed by a German U-boat 11 miles from shore. Rescue efforts were mounted and 761 people were saved.

Back in time Cobh also served as an emigration point for those seeking a new life in America, and a statue of Annie Moore stands on the waterfront. She is believed to be the first person to be processed at Ellis Island in New York in 1892.

Dominating the harbour skyline is St Colman's Cathedral with its 100 metre-high spire. It forms a towering backdrop to the picturesque buildings that hug the shoreline. The cathedral, which took 46 years to construct, houses a 49-bell carillon, the largest in Ireland.

# Valentine's Gifts

## by Kitty-Lydia Dye

WHEN I first arrived in the village of Aldeby, the name Jack Valentine would cause a shiver to run down my spine. Could the spirit possibly be real?

I pictured a shadow of a man stretched by the noon sun, his tapered fingers creeping around the door. No discernible features or clothes, besides the impression of a sharp grin and a top hat and tails. His long legs would be bent to send him leaping over cottages, leaving behind his ghastly gifts.

My vision of him seemed a lot like Spring-Heeled Jack, the phantom who haunted London. Perhaps he had moved to the countryside.

I'd been working in the dairy the day I heard about him. My mistress's sons were nearby, conspiring as usual. There wasn't much to occupy a person while churning, so I had long ago lost my shame over listening in on interesting conversations.

"Jack Valentine will be making his rounds soon," Joshua was telling his brother.

Harry laughed.

"I bet Sarah will get a shock! She'll be starting at every branch knocking against her window."

What on earth were they talking about? Curious, I had glanced over my shoulder to gauge their expressions. They caught me.

"Interested, Emma?" Joshua joked. "I bet you're hoping for a visit from him as well."

"Certainly not! I don't know such a man." I was a respectable girl.

"He's not –" Joshua made to explain, then Harry nudged him.

"He's as old as the trees," Harry warned me. "A spirit who frolics around Norfolk the night before Valentine's Day. Always up to mischief, especially when it concerns pretty young maids."

Then they strolled away, slapping one another's backs, leaving me to consider what such a creature would want with me.

A week had gone by, and still my imaginings plagued me.

Set in 1850

Illustration by iStock.

Something tugged at the back of my dress. I started, then realised with relief who it was.

"What is it, Lily?"

My younger sister huddled against my side, looking to me for reassurance. I was barely sixteen, yet I was all she had.

I ruffled her hair, still churning with my other hand.

"Don't be afraid. They were only sheep!"

We'd never seen one so close before. There was plenty in this village that was going to be new for us.

Lily shook her head.

"There's so much sky and grass. It doesn't smell like home!"

I looked out of the lattice window, gazing across endless flat fields. I breathed in, coughing from the strong odour of manure on the fields. There was something else, so faint, almost like sipping water: fresh air.

Back in London, it was steel and smog, harsh-flaring lantern light or storm-cloud darkness. The softness of the daylight coming into the dairy, pale as gossamer, was unfamiliar.

I glanced at the thatched roof and saw the clear sky through the ventilation hatch. The stones of the walls were uneven and rustic.

The city was always racing ahead to be more modern, and here it felt as if I had fallen into the past.

Panic gripped me. What would our life be like now? What would become of my sister and me? I knew nothing of this place.

I swallowed and pushed down my worries. It did not matter what I feared; Lily needed me. I would have to be strong.

"Will Aubrey follow soon?" Lily asked.

My grip around the churn crank tightened, my jaw ached.

"Aubrey has to make his own way. He'll do well in the Navy."

Our brother had abandoned us to furnish his own career. What would our parents have said? They were gone, drowned in a steamboat accident.

The workhouse found some use for us. A high-born lady had set up a dairy in the country on a charitable whim, and young girls were trained for suitable prospects.

"Go on," I whispered, nudging Lily. "You need to scald the pails."

I glanced at the other girls working. Most were turning the casks as I was, while some scrubbed the floors or sieved cow hairs out of the milk.

All their faces were pinched tight, cheeks pale, eyes watery bright with hope and unease.

I did not want to see such expressions reflected at me, so instead I looked outside. Men were in the fields, tools glinting from the orange sunlight as the soil was ploughed.

They were nothing more than shadows hunched over, as though tied to the land.

I'd been up well before cock crow. The room smelled faintly of old spilt milk, no matter how much we cleaned. Hot sunshine beat upon the men, but in here the shade of the trees kept the heat at bay. Only my feet felt cool, though.

Not too fast, not too slow – it was frustrating how much effort was required to churn just right. Having to be quick, yet lurching to a stop just before it really ran away from me.

I gripped the crank so tight it left an imprint on my hand.

I couldn't make a mistake. There were plenty of other girls in the workhouse desperate for my job.

The cask that the crank was attached to turned, milk and half-formed butter sloshing within. The uniform I wore was a full-length white dress and cap starched into stiffness.

I enjoyed lifting the lid once the butter was ready and I had to get rid of the excess milk. The butter had a sweet smell, the colour of it a pale yellow, tempting me to sail my finger through and have a taste.

Singing drifted by, strong and rough. Ever so slightly, my turning slowed.

I was looking for Bernard, although it would be impossible to tell apart those shadow figures. I felt foolish, being entranced by a song. Yet the singing helped me forget the faint ache of my arms, and let me dream a little.

Bernard was about my age. My eyes followed him when I passed him each morning on the way to the dairy, caught by the determined set of his jaw and the way his mouth twitched, parted as though he meant to speak, as he considered an obstacle in his path. He seemed to exude warmth.

Pale hair, tied back out of his face. Thick eyebrows; dark, narrowed eyes. Each movement as he swung his hoe was thought out, assured, rather than a flailing swing.

I thought he must be the cowkeeper's son, as the closest I had been to him was when it was my turn to help with the milking.

As I heaved up the pails, I saw Bernard fussing the cows, cooing so thickly in his accent I hadn't a clue what he was saying, but they certainly looked content. I doubt I had more than a glance from him, but the gentleness that belied his strong physique intrigued me.

It was shameful for a dairymaid to consider such things.

The figures drew away as they went further up the field. I sang as well. I was remembering a bird who used to appear at the bedroom window of the workhouse, a crafty gleam in its eye.

I had seen plenty of magpies since arriving here, but none were like my magpie. Out of everything, I missed him the most.

Quickly, I ducked my head, cheeks hot. The dairy door had opened and the lady came in. We left our churns, lining up so that our hands could be examined for cleanliness.

My mind should not be wandering. If I worked hard, I could give my sister a better life.

I did not mind the work. I preferred being kept busy. However, there would be no chance for fun. A faint shudder of weariness went through me. A workhouse girl was always on edge, having to ensure others saw her as respectable or else she was sent away.

* * * *

Valentine's Eve arrived. The dairymaids lodged with the lady's old nursemaid, Mother Gerrie, in a cottage in the manor grounds, far away from any other buildings.

The rustling of the leaves and bushes, followed by the harsh clacking of blackbirds, made me tense. My sister nestled beside me, and the room murmured with the others' snores. Yet it was still too quiet.

Shadows of the trees' spindly branches fell upon us, consuming the round orb of the moon. I lay there, cold no matter how tightly I held myself, eyes wide at the howling shriek of a hunting owl.

Somehow, I managed to sleep.

When I stirred, Lily was gone. I jolted up, panicked, then I heard her excited chatter coming from the kitchen.

Of course, breakfast. Food was the only thing to motivate us both.

That morning's brief rain spell still spattered the window, sunlight glimmering on the droplets. No unwelcome visitors had come calling last night.

Then a gloved hand appeared and rapped hard. I shrieked, holding my blanket up to shield my nightdress.

How dare someone try to spy upon me asleep! I rushed out, dashed aside the curtain and opened the window.

The man was gone. All that remained was a blackberry-stained package wrapped in twine.

My hand hovered, not quite daring to touch. It must be some cruel prank because I was an outsider. Most likely it was the lady's sons playing tricks again!

They'd probably fished an eel out of the Broads. That was what I thought as I carefully pulled the package open, even though it was not the right shape.

A straw doll the size of my thumb lay there, fashioned into a girl wearing a scrap of white cloth that, I assumed, was supposed to resemble my dairy dress. A pink ribbon was wrapped around her waist. My heart hammered in horror – it must be a poppet!

Before I could examine it further, Mother Gerrie called for breakfast. I changed and hurried into the kitchen to find my sister at the table, covetously clutching a handful of sweets.

As I helped Mother stir the porridge, the doll tucked in my apron pocket, I asked who had given them to her.

"That'll be Jack Valentine," Mother Gerrie said. "He came in the night and left something for all the girls here. You've got a few sweets as well."

Mother Gerrie winked at me. I remembered, weeks ago, seeing her leaving market with a sweet jar in her basket.

"Jack Valentine's such a giving soul, always finding a little gift for everyone."

"Valentine gives presents?" I asked. "Good ones?"

"Of course! He's a fairy spirit for Valentine's Day. He's nothing but teasing and affection. Why'd you think he was anything different?"

I flushed, not wanting to admit what the lady's sons had told me. Instead, I showed her the doll.

"That's a mighty fine gift, a corn dolly from the last harvest. Lucky girl. And look, there's a message."

Tucked under the white cloth was a scrap of paper.

*My sweetheart, you'll not know my name, but you are very dear to me. Each day I work in the fields, I hear you singing with the birds. But there is also sadness in your voice. Do you miss your old life?*

*I am not one for mardling. I lose my tongue with you around.*

*If you accept my courting, I've hidden another gift amongst the sheep.*

*– Jack Valentine.*

My work in the dairy awaited. I set off with the others and, as we always did, walked past the sheep field. I must not look for the second gift. It would get me in trouble. I stared resolutely ahead.

Surely whoever was trying to court me would not pester the poor creatures to tuck a message in their wool? My estimation of him would fall quickly, if so.

The sheep stared at me balefully, their lazy expressions making me think they knew something I didn't.

Did I want to discover who this sweetheart was? I had my sister's future to think of. We were not brought here to flirt and find husbands.

Yet my curiosity sparked. The fluttering in my chest was something I barely recognised – excitement. I wanted some fun.

Too long had I taken on the role of mother. I wanted just one day to be a girl, dreaming of adventure and kisses.

There, upon the gate, was a recent carving of a ram. Beneath that, hanging from another ribbon, dark red this time, was a pouch.

It held another message, alongside a few polished pebbles that were a pale blue and chipped in an almost heart-like shape.

*I'd face down Black Shuck and his evil eye for you. I want to sit with you in church and whisper all the folktales hereabouts. I want you to love this place as I do and never leave. The last gift is tucked away somewhere I am always considered to be hiding. Jack Valentine.*

My secret admirer could be anyone – even someone I did not know. I had certainly caught their attention.

Out of everyone, the person I wanted it to be was Bernard. He was the only lad I fancied spending time with, although all I knew was his singing voice and laughter.

The final gift was amongst the roots of the oak tree that shaded the dairy. I scuffed away the crumbling dry soil, expecting another ribbon.

Tucked in the fallen leaves was a wooden carving. It looked so real. He had carved the magpie I so often sang about. The bird I missed.

An admirer I did not know, yet he understood me so well.

I sniffed and felt wetness gleam upon my eyelashes.

I had thought I would never find a home here, terrified I might be sent back, unable to settle. If this admirer was willing to welcome me, might I have a chance at starting a new life?

I tucked the bird into my pocket and kept my hand closed around it for good luck.

I approached the cowshed, listening. Bernard's voice drifted, lilting and gentle. He was brushing down one of the cows. Sweat glimmered on his brow from working the fields earlier and his cheeks were ruddy from the sun.

I watched him a while, getting up my nerve. We were no more than strangers. Yet I would drive myself mad wondering.

"Mr Valentine?" I called and saw him start, the brush going slack.

"And what do you want with me, Miss Emma?" he said, voice light with playfulness.

"I wanted to thank you for the gifts."

He cocked his eyebrow.

"I'm afraid I don't know –"

He trailed off as I went on tiptoe and brushed my lips over his cheek, tickled by his sideburn.

"I would prefer to meet my Valentine, rather than have him run away," I told him. "Walk with me tomorrow morning after church?"

He nodded, speechless but grinning, and went back to his work. I returned to the dairy, humming.

I would have to be careful. There was every possible chance Bernard would turn out to be someone I could not love.

Nevertheless, the thrumming in my chest could not be stilled. Finally I felt as though I had settled in this place.

I would enjoy discovering who my Jack Valentine truly was. ■

# The World Outside

## by Jessma Carter

THE van was still cold. Andrew had been up before five and was using the radio to keep him alert. The fish market had been its usual raucous self, but that was a noise he could blot out. He had concentrated on finding the best fish for his customers. Arbroath smokies were always popular. Andrew smiled to himself. Mrs Mackintyre would be pleased.

She wouldn't say much. She'd just look at him and ask, "Ony smokies the day?" and then dig into her purse for the money.

Andrew drove on and pulled into the side of the road beside Mrs Mackintyre's cottage. He sounded his horn and waited.

There was a lot of waiting sometimes but Andrew found it quite pleasant. He had photographs of his wife and daughter taped on to the dashboard and a Thermos of tea to take when he reached the village.

He hummed along with the music and waited. Maybe Mrs Mackintyre hadn't heard him, so he ambled out of his van and walked up to the front door and rang the bell.

When there was no reply, he drove down to the village.

"She's off again. That's where she is. I heard as how it was somewhere in England. I think she said the Cotswolds." Mrs Murphy offered her opinion with a resigned sigh.

\* \* \* \*

It had all started three winters ago when the snow was deep on the ground. It was the first winter since Jenny Mackintyre's husband had died.

Jenny had slept badly, stumbled up, then wrestled with her back door in order to fetch some coal for her fire.

The door had always been loath to open when it was cold and wet and she had to push it hard, but she pushed it so hard that it swung wide, propelling her on to the ground.

It took her a while to struggle back inside and get to the telephone.

*Illustration by David Young.*

Dr Kerr was a good-natured lad, Jenny had to admit, although she didn't much like his advice.

"I'll get the nurse to call in tonight and give you a hand getting into bed. In the meantime, put as little weight as you can on that ankle.

"No need to be distressed. You'll be fine if you take care when you move. Have you a walking stick?"

"A nurse! Don't say nurse to me! I can manage fine!" Jenny was near tears, whether in frustration or annoyance it was difficult to tell.

However, she had a deep-rooted respect for doctors and decided to make no further protest.

The nurse, when she came, was a surprise to Jenny. She was young and pretty and made her laugh – not at all like the district nurse.

Her name was Ginty – no, not short for anything, just Ginty, and she was from England. She made a good cup of tea and remembered just how much milk and sugar to put in.

"You're English, then, Ginty?" Jenny asked.

Ginty laughed.

"I'm English and I come from England and I'm happy to be here in Scotland."

"What brought you here, then?"

"Love." Ginty gave Jenny's pillow a good plump up. Jenny was settled, ready for a story while she had her tea. She looked at Ginty expectantly.

"He was in bed when I met him."

Jenny smiled.

"There's not many can say that without a blush. Tell me more."

"He's a runner. He had broken his leg and he was the worst-tempered man I had ever met. He was furious with himself."

"But he must have improved – in temper, I mean – for you to end up talking about love."

"You could say so, and if you behave yourself, Mrs Mackintyre, I'll show you photographs of him and where we are to be married."

For a contented fortnight, Ginty helped Jenny for an hour in the morning and an hour in the evening.

It was summer, the nights were long and light, and Jenny looked intently at the photographs that Ginty showed her.

"That's the Lake District, then? It was on these hills that he broke his leg? It's as bonnie as Scotland," she said.

"You've never been there?"

"No. I've never had time or money to travel much."

Jenny was silent as she lifted the photographs to the window. The light was fading but she could still see the hill behind her house and could imagine hills beyond and beyond.

"Is the Lake District far?" Jenny asked presently.

Ginty shook her head.

"You can go by bus or train from Edinburgh. Ian, my fiancé, is back in Scotland, but we often go down to my home in Keswick," she answered.

Jenny Mackintyre had never been idle. She had learned in the early years of marriage that if she didn't take care then the dust sidled in.

She had no washing machine, just a scrubbing board and elbow grease, and now here she was in the 1950s, resting on a couch, frustrated and bored and, for the first time in her life, she had spare money in the bank. The money her husband had put into a policy was poor exchange for his presence and it had lain untouched for more than a year.

Jenny thought of it as she listened to Ginty.

"I have a mind to travel," Jenny said thoughtfully. "I feel fit and ready to go, and now that I've got back the use of my legs, I should make the most of them. The Good Lord didnae give me legs to lie about here."

Ginty laughed.

"Well, this is my last visit. I hope to see you around, of course, but I'm pleased you're fit and well." She brought a package out of her bag.

"Here's a calendar with pictures of the Lake District. You have a look at that and see if you don't think it's just as beautiful as Scotland."

∗　∗　∗　∗

"Your problem, Mum," Jenny's daughter Esme said, "is that you don't know how to rest.

"Whyever would you go off on your own to Keswick?"

"I won't be on my own. Not for a minute. I'll be in a bus or in a hotel or sight-seeing with other people."

"Let me take you into Edinburgh and see you on the bus, at least," Esme offered. "I'll feel reassured when I see who you're travelling with."

Apart from a young couple from Germany, the people on the bus tour were middle-aged to elderly.

Jenny approved; after all, who would choose to drive when you could sit on these cosy seats and look out on the scenery both left and right?

She was seated near the front of the bus beside a woman from Perth whose two friends were across the aisle.

Conversation was easy and, as Jenny found out, people open up a bit when they're talking to somebody they know they will probably never meet again.

"I just had to get away," her neighbour confided. "He reads the paper out loud every night. Every night. He seems to think I cannae read for myself."

"That's men for you," her friend agreed from across the aisle. "I come for a change. There's nothing like a change to set you up for emergencies." She leaned towards Jenny. "On your own, are you?"

"It's the first time I've been on a bus holiday, but I'm used to being on my own."

"We'll look out for you at meal times. Nice to have someone to talk to. It's talking that keeps us going." It was Meg from Falkirk who spoke.

She was a cosy-looking woman with a warm smile. Jenny relaxed as the bus and its passengers travelled south.

*　*　*　*

Ten days later Jenny was home, exchanging her opinions with Esme.

"I'm not tired tired, if you know what I mean. I've been real busy, talked a lot, seen a lot." She reached into a canvas shopping bag and brought out a handful of leaflets and calendars.

"Look here. This is what we did; this is where we went. There's a lot of lakes down there. And hills.

"And you can visit the homes of poets and storytellers. Wordsworth and Beatrix Potter. Just let me get my breath back and I'll tell you more."

"And you managed to walk around all right? No problems with those legs of yours?" Esme asked.

"None. I had too much else to think about. Do you know the folks down there have never heard of an Arbroath smokie? They said they knew about kippers, though."

Esme was relieved. Perhaps her mother would be content for a while. She would be happy to reminisce as she looked through her calendars and postcards.

"And look here." Jenny brought out a notebook from her handbag. "Look at the addresses I've got of some of the people I met.

"I said I'd keep in touch and I'll keep my promise. There were all sorts on the bus. Even an American preacher. He had toured Scotland before he got on the bus for the Lake District, but he said he'd like to know more. He turned out OK, even although he was chock full of hallelujahs."

∗  ∗  ∗  ∗

Two months later, Jenny was off again – this time to the Yorkshire Dales.

"I met some lovely people," she said to her daughter when she came back home, "and I liked the way they called me 'flower'."

She produced a bundle of leaflets from her bag.

"When you've got a minute, I'll tell you about those places."

Esme smiled, relieved to see her mother back home and with lots to talk about.

Soon Jenny's home was filling up with reminders from other parts of Britain – a shell from a beach in Brighton, a woollen shawl from the Cotswolds, a little painted pot from Stafford, plus many, many leaflets.

"I've been thinking," she said to Esme one day.

Esme looked at her mother's face and felt a groan coming on. What was her mother going to suggest now?

"You know how they say that travel broadens the mind?"

Esme waited.

"Well, I was thinking maybe I could invite some of my new friends here. I was thinking maybe I could clean out those two bedrooms upstairs that you and your brother had."

Esme was surprised and delighted.

"I'll give you a hand. I think that's a great idea. I'll enjoy meeting new people as well."

"You approve?" Jenny sounded hesitant.

"Of course, Mum. Write down all the things you would like to do and have never done. All the places you would like to see."

"I've already done it!" Jenny fumbled in her bag.

*Go somewhere I've never been at least once a year.*
*Try making bread.*
*Read "Jane Eyre".*
*Learn how to tap dance.*
*Learn to ride a bike.*

Esme shook the list and began to laugh.

"What gave you the idea to do all these things?"

"Because when I went away on my own to England, it was the first time I had ever been anywhere new on my own. And it's true what they say: travels broadens the mind. It gave me notions."

The following morning, Jenny was ready for Andrew, the fishman.

"I've been thinking, Andrew, maybe you could bring a few scallops and prawns one of these days?"

"I could, Mrs Mackintyre. Gone off Arbroath smokies, have you?"

"No, not at all, Andrew. I'll be giving them to some of my guests soon enough. But I like a bit of a change now and again. Just now and again, to keep me abreast of what's ado in the world." ■

**M**GM'S family drama "The Yearling" captured the hearts of audiences in 1946 in what proved to be its most successful – and expensive – film of that year. It cost over $4 million to make and required over 400 animals, 32 of which, including five fawns, had to be specially trained.

Adapted from the Pulitzer-prize-winning novel by Marjorie Kinnan Rawlings, it tells the story of an impoverished farming family in post-civil-war Florida, and their only surviving son, Jody, who adopts a young fawn as a pet after its mother is shot.

Jody is devoted to Flag, the yearling of the title, but the fawn continually destroys the family's precious crops. Eventually, the boy faces a choice between saving his family or saving his friend. Audiences worldwide wept.

Gregory Peck and Jane Wyman played Jody's parents. The role of Jody was played by newcomer Claude Jarman Jr., who won the part over 19,000 other hopefuls.

It was the only film to be nominated for Oscars in both the Best Actor and Best Actress categories in 1947, the year in which it won the Oscar for Best Cinematography, Color.

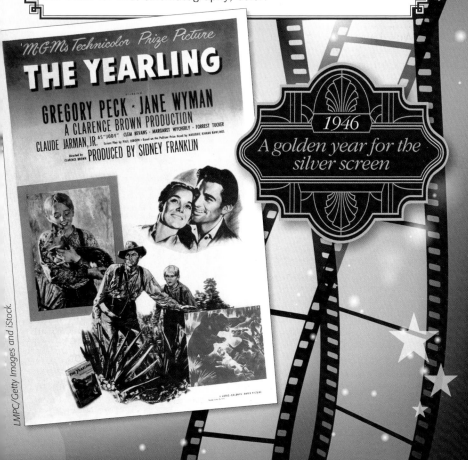

MGM's Technicolor Prize Picture

**THE YEARLING**

GREGORY PECK · JANE WYMAN
A CLARENCE BROWN PRODUCTION
CLAUDE JARMAN, JR. AS "JODY"   CLEM BEVANS · MARGARET WYCHERLY · FORREST TUCKER
Screen Play by PAUL OSBORN · Based on the Pulitzer Prize Novel by MARJORIE KINNAN RAWLINGS

PRODUCED BY SIDNEY FRANKLIN
Directed by CLARENCE BROWN

1946
A golden year for the silver screen

# An Easter Tail

## by Katie Ashmore

WHOA! Mum, what's that awful stink?"

Paula dropped her magazine and raced towards the kitchen. But it was too late. The smell of burning hit her as soon as she opened the door.

Eyes watering, she threw the charred remains of her cake into the sink.

She was opening windows when her husband, Jeremy, came in.

"How's it going?" He caught sight of the black mess oozing in the washing-up bowl. "Not so good, I see."

It was the Easter fair. Paula's friend, Alison, was organising the cake stall. This year, Paula had wanted to help. Really help.

Alison had always accepted her efforts with good grace – the sunken fairy cakes filled with icing to disguise deep craters, the toasted carrot cake and, worst of all, the muffins – well, the less said about them better.

No, this year she wanted things to be different.

"Hey, Mum, great cake!" Her teenage son, Sam, came into the room and looked at the smouldering remains, a massive grin spreading across his face.

He was soon followed by his sister, Becky.

"Aw, that's disgusting. You're not going to make us eat that, are you?"

"Haven't you kids got anything better to do than tease your mum?" Jeremy asked.

"Not really," Sam replied, his grin taking on Cheshire Cat proportions.

Jeremy raised an eyebrow.

"Well, in that case, you can do a few jobs for me. First, the car needs cleaning, second . . ."

But he didn't get any further. Sam was already halfway out the door.

"Er, sorry, Dad. Just remembered, um – homework!" he yelled as he disappeared upstairs.

Jeremy laughed.

"Works every time!"

"What about you, Becky?" Paula asked their daughter.

"I'll go and check on Jessica, if you like."

Jessica was their pregnant rabbit. They had looked after a friend's pet while they were on holiday, and the result was that Jessica was about to have a whole herd of Easter bunnies.

As she left, Becky gave Paula a hug.

"Don't worry, Mum, I'm sure the next lot of cakes will be OK. Perhaps you'll even win a prize!"

"Maybe a wooden spoon." Paula laughed.

Later that day, Paula's family were back in the kitchen, eyeing a batch of newly baked cupcakes with caution.

On this attempt, she'd actually produced something that was neither burned nor sunken, and with a swirl of yellow icing of which she was rather proud.

"Well, come on, then, who's going first?" she asked.

"I will," Jeremy said at last.

Sam slapped him on the back.

"Good for you, Dad. You're a hero!"

The kids watched with fascination as he bit into the cake. He grinned and attempted to rub his tummy, but then dashed, spluttering, to the sink.

Sam roared with laughter.

## Not A Morning Person

I am not a morning person
Just in case you haven't guessed,
I am not the sort of person
Who arises full of zest.
I loathe my old alarm clock,
And I'd throw it in the bin,
Except, of course, I need it still,
To stop me sleeping in.
So pass me, please, that coffee cup,
For let it not be said,
"She only comes awake, you know,
When it's nearly time for bed!"

Maggie Ingall.

"You've done it again, Mum! Awesome!"

"Hey, they're probably not that bad," Becky said, punching his arm.

Jeremy looked up, eyes streaming.

"Whatever did you put in them?" he asked.

"Just what the recipe said, you know – flour, butter, eggs, a tablespoon of banana flavouring . . ."

"Don't you mean a teaspoon, Mum?"

"No, I'm sure I – oh! Oh, dear."

Sam roared again.

"That's enough," Jeremy told him. He was sipping a glass of water and seemed to have recovered. "Stop gloating or I'll make you eat the lot."

"Why don't you two check on Jessica again while your dad helps me clean up?" Paula suggested.

But soon the kids were tumbling back into the kitchen.

"Mum, Dad, guess what! Jessica's had the babies and there's seven of them."

"Seven? Goodness, what will we do with so many rabbits?"

"Never mind that. Come and see them – they're gorgeous."

And they were. The sweetest little balls of fur imaginable, warm and snuggled up to their mother, and they had arrived in time for Easter.

Still, Paula reflected, there was no way they could keep them all. As the kids squabbled over them, she turned to Jeremy.

"The fair's tomorrow, I've nothing to take, and whatever will we do with all these bunnies?"

✳   ✳   ✳   ✳

Next morning, Paula woke with a sinking feeling and, for a moment, couldn't think why. Then she remembered – the Easter fair.

Jeremy was already up.

"Don't worry, love. I'll make you an Easter bonnet so you can enter the hat competition instead."

"Thanks, but are you sure that's a good idea?" She knew Jeremy wasn't renowned for his creative skills.

"Of course. When your bonnet wins, you won't worry about cakes any more!"

She wasn't convinced, but left him to it and went to ring Alison.

"How did it go, Mum?" Becky asked when she got off the phone.

"Fine," she mumbled.

"What's the matter?"

"Nothing. It's just . . . when I explained that I wouldn't be bringing cake this year, Alison actually sounded relieved."

Becky tried not to laugh.

"You probably imagined it, Mum. Anyway, she'll be glad of your help."

"I don't know. She's already got plenty of volunteers. I wish I could think of another contribution to make."

At that point, Jeremy strolled into the room, looking very pleased with himself. Sam followed closely behind.

"I've finished, love." He whipped a tea towel from the object he was holding. "Ta-da!"

There was stunned silence. Then Sam snorted with laughter and grabbed his phone.

"Put it on, Mum. Take a selfie."

Paula stared. It was more a crown than a bonnet, with what looked like an enormous squirrel on the front, straw glued haphazardly beneath it.

"What is it?" she asked weakly.

"It's Jessica," Jeremy replied. "Great, isn't it?"

Paula shook her head.

"Sorry, love, but I'm not going to wear that."

"Why not?"

It was Sam who answered.

"Come on, Dad. Just look at it!"

✳   ✳   ✳   ✳

The fair was nearly over. Paula could see Jeremy on the far side of the hall. It was impossible to miss him.

He had entered the hat competition himself and had insisted on wearing it all afternoon. It flapped above his head defiantly.

Everything had gone well. Jeremy and the kids were enjoying themselves and Paula was quietly proud of her own small contribution.

The cake stall had done a roaring trade and Alison was pleased with this year's efforts. Now it was time for the prizes.

Paula stood with her family and cheered as Alison went to collect the prize for best Easter cake. Next was the hat competition, won by Liz.

"This year, there's a booby prize," Rev. Tim announced. "The wooden spoon goes to Jeremy for his creativity and courageous hat modelling."

There was a burst of laughter and thunderous applause.

"I would also like to thank the winner of this year's most original stall," he continued, "and that's Paula. 'Guess the name of the rabbit kittens' has proved extremely popular.

"Not only that, but in a few weeks' time those kind families who have offered to give a good home to the kittens will be able to claim them."

At the last minute, she'd had a brainwave. Paula had taken photos of the babies and set up a stall.

She was finally a winner and, in addition, she had found safe homes for all of the babies to go to.

No-one cheered louder than her own family when she held up her prize – a book entitled "The Idiot's Guide To Baking". ■

# Flamborough Head, Yorkshire

The chalk headland on the Yorkshire coast attracts hikers keen to take in the beautiful coastal views and sea air. It's worth a visit to Flamborough Head Lighthouse, too – once you scale the 119 steps, the views from the top over Bridlington Bay and the heritage coast are magnificent. There are actually two lighthouses; the first, built by Sir John Clayton in 1674, is the oldest in existence, though it's not usually open to visitors. The newer lighthouse was commissioned in 1806.

Bempton Cliffs aren't far away and are home to more than 200,000 seabirds, including puffin and kittiwakes. You can also see an array of wildlife at nearby Danes Dyke nature reserve.

For a bit of history, Sewerby Hall and Gardens is worth a visit, and if you want a bit more hustle and bustle then Filey is along the coast from Flamborough Head and proves popular with tourists.

# Letitia's Lucky Day

## by Christine Bryant

THE small, slinky, black creature stared at Letitia through bright orange eyes, its tail flicking in time with her beating heart. A black cat.

That's fine, she told herself, that's good luck. She knew not everyone believed that, but she'd always considered them a good omen.

Letitia breathed a sigh of relief. Good fortune. Of course it was. It was hard to believe anything else of the gorgeous little bundle of fur in front of her.

She bent down to stroke it, and at that moment, a car drove through a nearby puddle, sending up spray that soaked her feet and made the cat scurry back into the undergrowth.

Lifting her boots, Letitia flicked off the water. So much for good fortune, she thought, and walked on.

There were plenty of puddles about this afternoon after the heavy downpour first thing, but now the few remaining grey clouds were scudding across the sky in the light breeze.

As she walked along, the comforting glow of spring sunshine peeped out occasionally from between the clouds, sparkling in patches on the rain-soaked pavement.

Letitia took a deep breath of the fresh air and felt lifted, as she so often did on a mild, windy day. All right, she hadn't had the best start to her day, but maybe from here on in everything would pick up and go well.

As she walked, she thought about her morning. Luck-wise, it hadn't been the most auspicious of beginnings.

First, it was the salt. She'd reached towards the back of the cupboard for a new pot of jam, her sleeve had caught the salt and the whole jar had crashed to the floor.

Salt everywhere. For a moment, she'd just stood there, looking at it in

*Illustration by Sarah Holliday.*

horror – spilled salt.

Letitia remembered reaching for the dustpan and sweeping it up. A sudden feeling of panic washed over her. Had she remembered? Surely she had.

You're being ridiculous, she told herself, it's just a silly superstition. She knew the inner voice was right, but she still sighed with relief when she suddenly remembered throwing a pinch of the salt over her left shoulder.

Daft really, but she didn't need any more bad luck, not after she'd accidentally put the umbrella up indoors. There'd been a rumble shortly afterwards and the heavens had opened.

Coincidence, she told herself, pure coincidence.

Letitia set off again down the high street towards Shilling Lane. Out of the corner of her eye, she caught sight of the little black cat, which seemed to be following her down the street.

It really was a pretty little thing. Now she looked at it more closely, it was obvious it was only a young cat. It still had a silly, kittenish look about it.

"You should go home," she said. "You're too young to be near a road. Go on now, shoo!"

Letitia waved a hand at it. The kitten sat and looked at her, then started to wash its paws.

"I haven't got time to take you now," she said. The kitten continued to stare at her, unmoved and unmoving. "Oh, do go home."

To her relief, the kitten turned and bounced off in the opposite direction.

Picking up her pace, Letitia glanced at her watch. It was almost ten minutes to! She sighed. Why was it roads always seemed to be longer when she was late?

She glanced up at a new, rather large black cloud that was casually peering over her shoulder.

"Sorry I'm late," it seemed to be saying, "but I've got a whole lot of rain here that's just itching to come down."

Please, Letitia thought, not until I get to the café. Surely you can hold off until then. She risked another glance at the sky. The cloud was looming, but it wasn't overhead just yet.

Puffing slightly, she increased her speed and turned the corner into Shilling Lane. Set at the end, in the middle of beautifully sculptured gardens, stood the Four Leaf Clover, a popular village tea room and bakery.

It hadn't come as any surprise when Julie had suggested it as a meeting place. Julie's passion for all things cake and pastry related was well known.

Steve always said . . .

Letitia turned in through the lychgate. She didn't want to think about Steve right now.

Part of her wondered if it had been such a good idea to keep up her friendship with his sister, but Julie was such a dear and they'd been friends for so many years, long before her relationship with Steve, a relationship that had ended abruptly two years before.

Although she and Steve had parted as friends, it still hurt just a little when Julie had told her he was getting married.

At least, that's what she thought it was, but was it? Did she really miss Steve, or was she just lonely, envious of the companionship and happiness he'd found?

Her own life hadn't exactly blossomed with romance in recent months, Letitia thought ruefully.

The ring of her mobile jolted her out of her thoughts. Letitia glanced down at the screen.

Julie.

"Hello?"

"Tish? It's me, Julie. I'm so sorry, I'm not going to be able to make it today.

"Poor Mum's slipped on the step in the back garden and I think she's broken her ankle. I'm taking her to A and E. Can we rearrange for another day?"

"Oh, my goodness, poor Rose!" Letitia exclaimed. "Yes, of course we can rearrange, no problem."

"That's great, thanks." Julie sounded relieved. Then a thought occurred to her.

"You're not there yet, are you?"

"No," Letitia fibbed. "I'm in the high street. Don't you worry, Julie, I need to do some shopping anyway.

"Give my love to Rose and tell her I hope she's better soon. I'll text you later."

"You're a dear, Tish, thanks. Speak to you later."

The phone went dark.

Slipping it back into her handbag, Letitia stood at the top of the path and mulled things over.

She could turn on her heel, go back to the high street and have a look around the shops.

The village was looking glorious now with baskets and tubs of mixed spring flowers, and swathes of daffodils on the green. Her favourite cherry trees were bursting with buds, just waiting for Nature's signal to blossom.

Yes, that would be nice.

Or she could treat herself to a mouth-watering pastry in the Four Leaf Clover. How long had it been since she'd treated herself to anything at all? Too long, she reckoned.

A big, sticky pastry and a nice cup of tea. A simple thing, but they were always the most enjoyable.

She glanced back over her shoulder. The black cloud had lumbered a little further across the sky and now seemed bigger, blacker and more menacing than ever.

Letitia thought about the day so far. With the way her luck was going, it was definitely going to happen.

She'd be halfway to the high street, well away from any hope of a shop doorway, and whoosh! Cloud burst.

Mind made up, she slipped her bag over her shoulder and marched off down the path decisively. Sticky pastry, here I come, she said to herself as she went.

She almost tripped over the black kitten as it darted out from behind a tree and danced in and out of her feet.

"Oh, no! Why are you still here?" she said. "Well, I'm sorry, kitty, lovely though you are, I'm not taking you back to where I found you, because I know exactly what will happen. I'll be halfway there and –"

Letitia's next words were lost in a splutter as she inhaled a large mouthful of water.

As it happened, "cloud burst" hadn't even come close. Great drops of water assaulted her head, spread rapidly across her scalp and started to run down her face.

Oh, my goodness, it was going to be torrential . . .

Frantically, Letitia searched in her bag for her umbrella and finally found the handle. Slipping her fingers through the loop, she gave it a good hard yank.

For a moment, the umbrella refused to budge, caught on the inside pocket, then suddenly it shot out, sending her keys and a small, shiny object hurtling towards the ground.

With a dull, splintering sound, the mirror hit the cobbles and broke into several pieces.

Letitia stared at it in dismay.

Seven years' bad luck! What else could go wrong?

# Café Confusion

I met a good friend for coffee today,
We went into town, to a brand-new café.
"Two coffees," I said, but the waitress just sighed.
She took a deep breath and then quickly replied,
"Latte or mocha or maybe espresso?
Lungo, cappuccino or even ristretto?
A long black, a flat white or small macchiato,
Or perhaps you'd prefer a strong, sweet cortado?"
I thought for a minute then smiled as I said,
"I think maybe we'll just have two teas now
      instead!"

**Lily Christie.**

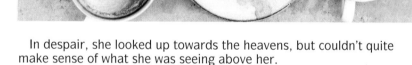

In despair, she looked up towards the heavens, but couldn't quite make sense of what she was seeing above her.

Metal rungs?

With a gasp, she realised there was a ladder over the door, propped against the wall.

She'd been so concerned with the smashed mirror that she'd walked right underneath it without even noticing. On top of everything else, she'd just walked under a ladder!

Could this day get any worse?

Letitia felt the unease returning as she tried to talk herself out of believing in another superstition, but the heavy cold drops that battered her head for a second time soon shook her out of it.

Then a voice broke into her thoughts.

"Oh, my goodness!"

Someone slid down the ladder to land beside her with a splash. The figure was young, clad in working gear and, Letitia couldn't help observing, quite attractive.

His face was concerned.

"Oh, no, I'm so sorry," he said, as a trickle of water dripped from her chin. "Are you OK? Oh, heavens, look how wet you are! I'll get you a towel . . ."

He darted indoors.

"I was just trying to clear the guttering a bit before the next lot comes down," he said when he returned, handing a clean, fluffy white towel to Letitia.

"The gutter's blocked and the water was pouring over the top earlier. I should have cleared the leaves out before it got as bad as this. I do apologise . . ."

He looked down in confusion and something glinting in the weak sunlight caught his eye.

Crouching down, he very carefully picked up all the shards of broken glass.

He looked up at Letitia.

"Oh, no, I'm afraid your mirror . . ."

As they surveyed the shattered remnants, Letitia could have sworn she saw his lips twitching with suppressed amusement.

He met her eye.

"I am sorry," he said again. "I can mend most things, but I suspect this has had it."

He grinned and Letitia couldn't help grinning back.

"That's fine," she said, taking the pieces from his hand and dropping them in a handy waste bin. "I was the one who dropped it. It's my own fault."

He smiled.

"Well, that's very understanding of you," he said, "but I can't help feeling a bit responsible.

"I wonder, would you allow me to buy you a cup of tea and some cake? You know, to make up for things?

"Some sort of compensation, almost . . . Oh, and my name's Graham, by the way."

Letitia found herself smiling. Compensation. What a perfect choice of word after the unlucky morning she'd had.

First the umbrella indoors, then the spilled salt, the little black cat, narrowly missingly getting soaked by a car, poor Rose's fall, their cancelled lunch, walking under a ladder, her broken mirror and now a soaking!

Maybe she could qualify for a place in the Guinness Book of Records – did they have a category for Unluckiest Person? If so, she was surely in with a shout!

Graham held out his hand and Letitia took it.

"I'm Letitia."

Graham's eyebrows rose in surprise.

"That's such a pretty name," he said. "Actually, my gran was called Letitia, believe it or not. Mum says I'm very like her."

He laughed.

"Maybe she's right, as well. Apparently, she was inclined to be a bit clumsy, too . . ."

Letitia chuckled.

"Well, none of us is perfect," she said, thinking how superstitious she was.

She glanced up at him. He was looking straight back at her. His eyes were a rich brown, the colour of Mother Earth, eyes that said warm, steady and reliable.

He waved a hand in the direction of the café.

"Shall we?"

Letitia shivered in her wet things and cast a longing look towards the cosy interior.

"It's very kind of you, but please, don't feel you have to . . . I should have been looking where I was going."

Graham looked at her steadily, a half-smile on his face that made her feel flustered.

'I'd like to," he said simply.

Letitia smiled.

"Then thank you. I can't deny that a hot cup of tea would be very nice."

"Wonderful." He stepped towards the ladder. "Just give me a minute till I move this thing, though," he said. "It might be dangerous to leave it here if people are passing by."

He pulled a face.

"We certainly don't want any more accidents, do we? Some just people don't like them at all.

"Mum can never bring herself to walk under ladders. Doesn't bother me personally, but some people swear by their superstitions, don't they?

"I suspect my mum would have had a fit if she'd walked under that ladder and then broken a mirror right after! She probably wouldn't have left the house for the next five years!" Graham roared with laughter and Letitia joined in half-heartedly.

"I don't give that nonsense a second thought myself," he continued cheerfully.

"Nor me," Letitia agreed robustly, crossing her fingers behind her back and praying her nose wouldn't grow.

"Especially today," he said, as they stepped into the warmth of the tea room.

"Today?" she queried, only half listening as she divested herself of her wet coat.

Graham nodded.

"I have a friend who won't go outside the door on Friday the thirteenth."

Letitia slid slowly into the seat he offered at a cosy table by the window.

Friday the 13th? Today was Friday the 13th?

Of course! She smiled to herself. Suddenly it was all clear. No wonder she had faced disaster after disaster this morning! What else could she have expected?

And people said superstitions were nonsense!

She settled comfortably into the seat and beamed up at Graham. Her world made sense again.

"Two teas coming right up," he said. "By the way, I don't suppose you've seen a little black kitten around, have you?" ▪

FILMED in black and white, this French retelling of the story of "Beauty And The Beast" was a masterpiece by director Jean Cocteau. The film employed hitherto unseen special effects, with settings based on paintings by Vermeer and drawings by nineteenth-century artist and engraver Gustave Doré, as well as sumptuous costumes by designers Christian Bérard and Marcel Escoffier. So complicated was the Beast's leonine make-up that it took five hours to apply before actor Jean Marais could begin his performance. During his 13-hour working days, the actor could not take solid food for fear of dislodging the Beast's distinctive fangs.

Taglined "The Picture of 1001 Wonders", the classic tale of the misshapen and misunderstood Beast, growing to love and be loved by the dutiful and open-hearted Beauty, played by Josette Day, is a beautifully made romantic fantasy that would have been a true escape from the realities of the physical and economic effects of the war in its immediate aftermath.

The film is a classic of French cinema and won the Grand Prize of the Cannes Film Festival in the year of its release.

MINERVA Films

JEAN MARAIS
JOSETTE DAY
MARCEL ANDEÈ
MILA PARELY
NANE GERMON
MICHEL AUCLAIR

Mise en scène de
JEAN COCTEAU

La Belle et la Bête

1946
A golden year for the silver screen

# Round The Maypole

## by Jean Robinson

FLORRIE stood at the lattice window surveying the land before her: the gardens, the farm and the woodlands beyond. All this should rightly be hers. Yet Fate had decided otherwise.

Her gaze fell on the maypole on the lawn below the window, bedraggled now, its ribbons rippling on the breeze in trails of faded purple and yellow.

Her mind drifted back to the times when, as a child, she'd come up to the big house with her brother and all the village children for the annual tea parties. Her brother's short trousers had been neatly patched, and his black boots shone. And both had been scrubbed to within an inch of their lives.

There had been pride but an underlying sadness in her mother's smile as she'd waved the two of them off.

It was at one of these tea parties that Florrie had first met Phillip, the only son of Squire Geoffrey who owned the big house.

Phillip always joined in the games at the tea parties. Once, when she'd fallen over and grazed her knee, Phillip had taken her to the big house and waited while one of the servants bathed and bandaged it.

After that he'd sought her out each year and made sure she had more than her fair share of all the goodies.

She'd asked her mother if Phillip could come to visit their small cottage one day.

"Goodness, no," Elsie had snapped. "We don't mix with high and mighty. Don't you start getting ideas above your station."

She'd sometimes see Phillip around the village, and he'd stop and talk to her. Over the years he grew more reserved and would give her a shy smile and quickly look away.

It seemed strange at first, but she didn't mind really because she knew his smile was still specially for her.

Well, she'd come a long way from the little girl who'd danced round

*Illustration by Helen Welsh.*

the maypole on that sunny afternoon.

She could remember staring up at the old red brick house, daydreaming about what it would be like to live in such a place, not realising that in only a few years she would know. As soon as she'd left school her mother had whisked her up there and managed to get her employed as kitchen maid.

How shocked she'd been at the way Philip changed. If they came across each other in the house, he would pretend he hadn't seen her and pass quickly on his way.

When she'd mentioned it to Cook, the portly woman had explained that it was "as it should be".

"But why? We've been friends since we played together at the tea parties!" Florrie exclaimed.

Cook turned away from the dough she was kneading and wiped her hands down the sides of her apron.

"He's the squire's son and you're a servant. You watch your step, my girl, or there'll be trouble." She waved impatiently towards the big stone sink. "There's pots to be scoured. No more of this nonsense."

Florrie had sighed deeply and rolled up her sleeves. It was true. Why would someone like Phillip consider a lowly kitchen maid as a friend?

During his years up at Oxford she'd seen little of Phillip, and when she came across him one day in the vinery, he seemed like a stranger. Gone was the awkward teenager. Before her stood a tall young man, hair sleeked back, blue eyes shining.

Yet he still had that same shy smile and reserved manner Florrie found so endearing. They'd passed some pleasantries and he'd quickly left.

How proud her mother would have been if she'd lived to see her now. From kitchen maid to housekeeper.

That had set a few tongues wagging within the household, but she'd held her head high and determined to prove she was worthy of the title.

The old grandfather clock in the hall began its sonorous chime, bringing her out of her reverie, and Florrie turned away from the window. She had work to do.

Yet her mind was troubled still, as memory stirred again of the moment she had learned of her true identity.

It was several months now since Squire Geoffrey had summoned her to his death bed.

"Please do not exert yourself," she'd pleaded as she saw how he struggled to speak. Gently she had taken his hand and put her ear close to his mouth to make it easier for him.

"My dear, there is something I have to tell you, something I should have told you long ago. My dear wife, Constance, could not bear a child. We adopted Phillip when he was a baby." He paused a moment as he gasped for breath.

"When your mother told me she was expecting you, it was not possible for her to stay in service here. I provided for her. It was not enough. But it was all I could do."

Florrie held her breath and squeezed his hand a little tighter. What was he telling her? Slowly the significance of his words began to dawn on her.

"Florrie, you are my only child," he breathed as he drifted into his final sleep.

Back in her room she'd sat and stared at the wall as the pieces fell into place. She'd often asked her mother who her father was and why her brother had a different one but had received no answer.

Florrie began to understand now how they had been able to live so well in their tiny cottage, never short of food or logs for the fire.

It explained the squire's kindness when she'd started work as a lowly kitchen maid, and why, when his wife had died, he'd immediately promoted Florrie to housekeeper.

How her mother must have suffered over the years, never telling a soul, loyally keeping his secret for all time.

Then yesterday, just three months after Squire Geoffrey had died, Phillip had approached her as she was sitting in the rose garden taking a breath of air after checking a large delivery of goods for the kitchen.

"I caught sight of you from the library window so took this opportunity." He hesitated. "I need to talk to you."

"Of course," Florrie said, getting up.

Something in Phillip's tone made her uneasy. Usually when he had something to discuss, he came straight out with it. Their easy friendship had soon been restored once he had taken over the estate.

They began to stroll along the path between the beds of roses. After continuing in silence for some way, he stopped and turned to her.

"Florrie, we've known each other for a long time."

"Why, yes," she replied, puzzled.

"And we have a good relationship?"

"Of course, Phillip. Why do you ask?"

"I think we work well together in running this place, would you agree?"

"Yes, I feel we do. Is there a problem I am not aware of?"

"No, no." He was quick to reassure her.

"Then what is it?"

Phillip stood uncertainly before her.

"There is something I wish to ask you." He was regarding her intently now. "Florrie, will you marry me?"

Florrie gasped and stared at him.

"Phillip, this is very sudden."

He moved uneasily from one foot to the other.

"Yes, I should not have sprung it upon you. And, of course, you must take your time to consider."

Then, to her dismay, he gave her a respectful nod and walked away, leaving her staring after him.

Florrie's stomach was churning. It was what she had dreamed of, marrying the man she had grown to love. But he had never declared his love for her. And his proposal just then had lacked any romance.

Then it struck her – this would be a marriage of convenience. His father had obviously explained the situation to Phillip before he died.

Although she could have no claim on the estate due to the circumstances of her birth, Phillip would feel obliged to right the wrong. He was that sort of man.

On unsteady legs Florrie made for the woods surrounding the lake, her mind in turmoil. She began to consider what he had offered.

If she could accept the situation, she could have both Phillip and this magnificent old house. Instead of housekeeper, she would be mistress. He was a good, kind man. Yet she knew she could never contemplate a loveless marriage.

Florrie feared seeing Phillip next day. She did her best to avoid him, but he found her in the dining-room checking that Betsy, the housemaid, had cleaned the silver cutlery as she had asked her to do.

To her dismay he was formally polite. No further mention was made of his proposal the previous day and she assumed he had taken her hesitation as a refusal.

They discussed the forthcoming dinner to celebrate his birthday. He obviously felt he'd done his duty by her and, as she had turned him down, they could now resume their normal working relationship.

The day of the dinner party saw the kitchen staff in a flurry of excitement. It was the first family gathering since the old squire had died. Cook was beside herself worrying over every detail and giving everyone a hard time.

Florrie had gone down to the kitchen to check the final details.

"I hear you've been cavorting with the squire," Cook announced when she saw her approaching.

"Whatever do you mean?" Florrie asked, taken aback.

"Now, madam, don't you play the innocent with me. You watch your step, my girl. We don't want history repeating itself."

A little knot of fear twisted inside Florrie as she stared, dumbstruck, at Cook.

"There's been some goings on in this house, I can tell you. And it all ends in tears. So, you be warned."

Florrie picked up the menu for the dinner, hands trembling. She was fully aware that the "goings on" had involved her mother and Squire Geoffrey.

But she was shocked that Cook should speak of it to her in this way until she realised that Cook still thought of her as the young lass who had scrubbed the pans and peeled potatoes.

And how could she resent the motherly woman who had always kept a watchful eye on her?

"He asked me to marry him," Florrie said, suddenly wanting some reassurance that she had made the right decision.

Cook looked up from the bird she was plucking.

"I see!" There was a moment's silence. "Then you snap him up before he changes his mind. You won't get an offer like that again."

"But he doesn't love me," Florrie objected.

Cook tutted.

"Come on, girl. What are you asking for? The moon and the stars?"

"I'm asking for love. How can a marriage work without that?"

"A marriage of that kind can work very well," Cook told her.

"Not for me," Florrie said, tossing her head and flouncing out.

After that Florrie put all thoughts of romance from her mind and concentrated on organising the dinner party.

It was only after the guests had retired from the table, the men for their brandy and cigars, the ladies to gossip, that Florrie saw Phillip.

He was escorting Melissa Thornbury across the hall to the drawing-room as Florrie left the dining-room after checking the lamps had been safely extinguished. They were laughing together and chatting amiably. A stab of pain cut through her.

The following afternoon Florrie was seeking Walter in the garden when Phillip caught up with her.

He gestured to the wooden bench beneath the beech tree.

"Could we sit a while?" he asked.

Her heartbeat quickened as she nervously perched on the edge of the bench, wondering what was to come now.

"I wanted to thank you for making last night such a success," he said, as he positioned himself beside her.

"It was no trouble," Florrie answered matter-of-factly.

He seemed reluctant to go and yet conversation became difficult to sustain. Then she remembered something that had been forming in her mind for some time.

"Phillip, can we start the tea parties again for the village children?"

To her disappointment he shook his head.

"What would we do? I think we would struggle to entertain them. The garden has become rather neglected, the maypole is in ribbons and the swing is no longer safe."

Florrie jumped up and stood facing him.

"But all that could be fixed. Walter would tidy the gardens."

Phillip looked thoughtful.

"It would take a lot of organising."

"I could do it. I know every family in the village." Florrie could tell he was warming to the idea. "We could ask the parents as well. Make it an annual event for the whole village," she continued with enthusiasm.

Phillip sighed and the ghost of a smile touched his lips.

"You are still a village girl at heart."

The flurry of excitement she had felt was crushed instantly. Of course she was. Nothing could change that. She did not belong in the big house, not as anything other than one of the servants.

He stood up, suddenly master of the house again.

"I must see Walter. There appears to be a problem with the high field. The cattle may need to be moved to better pasture."

Florrie wandered back into the house, heavy-hearted. It would have been like this if they had married. Phillip still thought of her as a servant and was probably relieved that she had refused his offer of marriage.

∗   ∗   ∗   ∗

Much to her surprise Phillip caught up with her later as she was leaving the small office where she dealt with the household accounts.

"Florrie, I've given some thought to your plan. I think I like the idea, if you are sure you are able to do this. It will mean a lot of work."

Florrie assured him in as calm a voice as she could that she would manage it very well and that she was sure it would be a great success.

∗   ∗   ∗   ∗

The day of the tea party dawned bright and sunny. Everything was perfect. The staff had been keen on the event, thinking how nice it would be to have something to look forward to.

"You've done wonders," Phillip told Florrie.

Bunting was strung between the trees. The long wooden table Walter had erected was covered in lacy cloths. Pretty napkins had been folded. Dainty sandwiches and fairy cakes sat on doilies on cake stands. There were bowls of plums and strawberries and a large jug of fresh cream.

There were flagons of ginger beer and large jugs of fresh milk.

Florrie watched excitedly as families trundled up the hill, the boys kicking tufts of earth, the girls skipping daintily in their pretty dresses. She hoped all would go well.

She need not have worried. By mid-afternoon the party was in full swing. Children darted round the meadow, having devoured all the lovely food. Their mothers remained at the long table drinking tea and gossiping. The men had organised an impromptu game of cricket, and were now standing with their tankards of ale discussing farming matters.

Archie began a lively tune on his fiddle and, holding the yellow ribbon that had been her favourite as a child, Florrie began to skip in and out with the children. She was back in her childhood, dancing round this very maypole, her long floral skirt swirling around her.

The evening, when it came, was perfect. A beautiful harvest moon cast its golden glow over the fields. She sat quietly alone, drained after the exertions of the day. It had been a success. Phillip had enjoyed it.

Several couples were engaged in a lively dance and Florrie watched with envy. Then she saw Phillip walking towards her, and her heart began to beat faster. He perched on the bale beside her.

"You look worn out."

She smiled and nodded, keenly aware of his proximity.

"Everyone agrees it was a good idea. They want to know if we will do this again next year."

"And shall we?" she asked, turning to him.

"I think we have to." He seemed more relaxed tonight. They sat in companionable silence for a while.

"Do you remember when we were children at these parties?" he asked.

"I looked forward to them all year," Florrie confessed. "It was the only time we ever ate cake."

He turned to her, a look of concern clouding his face.

'Florrie, you look so sad. Can you not tell me what is on your mind?"

"I think you know the answer," she whispered.

"Because I asked you to marry me? I'm sorry I put you in that position. I felt our friendship had developed into something deeper."

"I thought you asked me out of duty because of my mother," she said.

"Why, what happened to your mother?"

Florrie stopped breathing as realisation dawned. He didn't know. His father had not told him. When she remained silent, Phillip took her hand. It felt warm and comforting and she did not pull away.

"Florrie, I asked you to marry me because I love you."

Before she knew it, she was in his arms and he was kissing her and then they were dancing round and round to the merry music.

When they were both out of breath he looked down at her, his arms still encircling her. He wasn't the squire any more. He was Phillip, her dear friend, the man she loved.

"But I can't change what I am," she warned him. "As you once told me, I'll always be a village girl at heart."

Phillip's smile was warm.

"It is what I love most about you, that you are so natural, so full of energy. The way you joined in the games. The children love you.

"Florrie, times are changing. We will make the future ours. Our love is all we need."

As his lips touched hers, all her doubts evaporated and, as his arms drew her close, she knew it was where she truly belonged. ■

# Tod Head Lighthouse

Opened in 1897, Tod Head Lighthouse, south of Stonehaven, was built by engineer David Alan Stevenson. Electrified in 1978, it provided a waypoint navigation between Montrose and Aberdeen up until it was decommissioned in 2007. It stands proud above a rugged headland and commands stunning views over the North Sea.

David Stevenson came from an esteemed family of lighthouse engineers. His grandfather, Robert Stevenson, built the Bell Rock Lighthouse – an incredible engineering achievement. In fact, the family were involved in constructing the majority of lighthouses in Scotland with works spanning more than 150 years, and their engineering feats have stood the test of time.

Another family member whose work has endured to this day is David Stevenson's cousin – Robert Louis Stevenson. Writing was obviously in the blood, as David's daughter, D.E. Stevenson, went on to become a best-selling Scottish author of historical romances.

# Animal
# Instinct

## by Teresa Ashby

FRAN was close enough to the café to smell the coffee when someone screamed. Her hand reached for the door, but she hesitated a moment too long, unaware in that instant that her life was about to change for ever.

She turned and saw a frightened dog running up to people, but once the woman screamed, everyone assumed the dog's intentions were bad. One man kicked out, missing the little Staffie by inches, and a woman waved her shopping bag at it.

"Stop!" Fran shouted, running back towards the dog. "She won't hurt you! What is wrong with you? Can't you see she's scared?"

"A scared dog is a dangerous dog," someone said.

"Here, girl," Fran said, crouching down and holding out her hand. "I won't hurt you. For heaven's sake, have none of you got dogs at home? What sort of way is that to behave? You're scaring her to death."

"Careful," a man said. "It might bite."

The dog recognised the friendly tone and flung herself at Fran.

Her fur was a beautiful blue and she wore a pink collar with two shiny tags dangling from it. Fran caught a glimpse of the name, *Valerie*, before the dog jumped to her feet and took off.

"Wait!" Fran called.

Not this, not today, she thought. She was meant to be meeting Cameron and she'd already let herself be delayed in the book shop.

Before she knew it, time had sped past. Rather like Valerie, who was now speeding away from her, swerving round people and buggies.

Fran looked back at the café, torn between keeping her date with Cameron and following the dog.

Valerie won. Cameron wasn't in danger of running in the road, or being snatched by some unscrupulous individual.

No doubt he'd have all the details he'd been collecting from estate

agents in a neat pile on the table beside him.

She suppressed a shudder and ran down the high street, wishing she hadn't put her phone in her bag. If she stopped to look for it, she would lose sight of the fleeing terrier.

There would be time enough to call Cameron once she'd caught Valerie, and then he'd understand. He loved dogs as much as she did.

He'd said when they moved in together they could get one, but it would have to be the sort that didn't shed. He didn't like mess.

Valerie stopped and looked back, her tongue lolling out of her mouth. When her gaze fell on Fran, she took off again, turning into an alley.

"Wait, I'm not going to hurt you," Fran called, ignoring the tuts of the Saturday afternoon shoppers. "Valerie!"

She ran round the corner then stopped, trying to catch her breath. Her shoes definitely weren't made for running.

Valerie stood at the far end of the alley watching her. It was as if she was waiting for Fran to catch up.

"Come here, Valerie!" Fran called. "I'm not going to hurt you."

She pulled off her shoes and started towards Valerie, who waited until Fran had almost reached her, then took off again towards the park.

Cars hooted as she sped across the road and Fran flinched, waiting for a bang, but by the time she got there, Valerie was on the other side.

This was one of the areas she'd hoped to live in, but Cameron was more interested in the new properties near the railway station. Handy for the commute to work, he said.

The new apartment blocks had swimming pools and gyms, balconies and lifts. But he'd promised to see what else was on offer in their price range when he went round the estate agents.

He spoke a lot about how two were able to live as cheaply as one, and how much money they would save by moving in together.

Fran worried about ground rents and service charges, but he said it was worth it to live somewhere decent. Old houses could be money pits.

He'd only decided they should live together the previous week and since then, Fran had felt her life was spiralling out of control, as if it wasn't her decision at all.

Valerie trotted across the park. She didn't seem to be losing any energy at all, whereas Fran's legs were aching and her cheeks burned. She struggled to draw in enough air.

"Can't you read?" a woman pushing a toddler in a buggy snapped. "Dogs must be kept on a lead in the park."

"She's not my dog," Fran protested, but the woman clearly didn't believe her.

Valerie went all the way to the other side of the park and came out by a row of tall terraced houses that glowed in the afternoon sun.

Once again the Staffie rushed across the road, causing cars to slam on their brakes and hoot furiously.

"Valerie?" A man walking a fox-red Labrador stopped in his tracks. He clearly recognised her, and she him. "What is it, girl? Has something happened to Alice?"

Fran arrived, panting and hardly able to speak.

"You know her?" she gasped. "Thank goodness. I've followed her all the way from the high street."

"What was she doing there?" He frowned. "Where's Alice?"

Valerie took off again, running down a narrow passage that led to the back of the terrace. The lane behind the houses was overgrown with brambles which caught and pulled at their clothes.

Then Valerie turned in through a gate and up to one of the houses. The back door was open.

"Hold Rufus for me," the man said, passing Fran his dog's lead. "Perhaps best you stay here while I look inside.

"It's OK, I'm a policeman and I know Alice well. I live next door."

Rufus wanted to follow, but when Fran told him to sit, he did so.

Now perhaps might be a good time to call Cameron.

"Where are you?" Cameron asked.

"Park Avenue."

"What are you doing there? I told you, I'm not interested in buying an older property."

"If you'd let me get a word in . . ." Fran said. "I don't think I'll be able to meet you this afternoon. There's been an incident."

"What sort of incident? Are you OK, Francesca?"

She was momentarily warmed by the concern in his voice.

"I followed a lost dog and I'm at her house. It seems something might have happened to the owner."

He sighed.

"Leave it to the police, Fran. Have you called them?"

"Actually, I'm holding the policeman's dog," she said, looking down at the Labrador and smiling. The dog wagged his tail in response.

"If the police are dealing with it, you don't need to be there," he said. "If you hurry, you can be back here in fifteen minutes. I really want to go through these properties so we can make appointments to view. I've already made a shortlist."

She'd been so close to walking into the café and planning the next stage of her life with Cameron. If it hadn't been for Valerie, she might well have been on her way to view a property at this very moment.

It was as if she'd come to her senses. As if worrying about a strange dog had freed her mind to make a decision she'd been avoiding.

Not once had Cameron said he loved her, and there was no romance involved in their decision to move in together. It was all financial and for the best, but it wasn't what her heart wanted.

Deep down she'd known that.

"Do any have gardens?"

She'd told him she really wanted a garden, even if it was only somewhere to arrange a few pots.

She heard him riffling through some papers.

"No. They're all apartments."

"We need to talk," Fran said, "and I can't do this over the phone."

He was silent for a moment.

"Do what?" he asked at last. "Are you breaking up with me? Just because I don't want a garden?"

"It's not just the garden, Cameron. It's everything. I don't think it's going to work. Us, I mean."

"I guess that's it, then," he said and while it felt like a relief, it also felt like a massive blow that he was able to let her go so easily.

"I'm sorry, Cameron."

"Don't be," he said. "Better now than further down the line."

"You're all right?"

"I'll be fine." he said and he sounded it. In fact, he sounded relieved. "To be honest, I can narrow my search down even more if I don't have to take your likes and dislikes into consideration.

"Moving in together was just a thought. I'll just have to look at something a bit smaller."

When the call ended, Fran stared at her phone in shock.

What had she done? What had Cameron let her do?

It was bizarre. She'd left home earlier with every intention of looking at properties with Cameron and here she was, standing in someone's back garden holding a policeman's dog and suddenly single.

And the worst part of all, she wasn't sad.

Maybe it hadn't hit her yet.

"You all right there?" Rufus's owner came out of the door. "I'm going to stay with Alice, but an ambulance is on the way. Could you maybe wait out the front and show them to the front door? I've unlocked it. Thank you –"

"Fran."

"Fran." He grinned. "I'm Matt and this is Rufus the Red. Valerie you've already met.

She made her way to the front of the house and waited for the ambulance, watching in dismay as Alice, looking very poorly, was carried out.

"Don't worry, Alice," Matt said. "I'll look after Valerie until you're better. I've called your daughter and she'll meet you at the hospital."

When the ambulance had gone, his shoulders slumped.

"I've never known this happen before," he said. "Usually, Valerie alerts her that she's going to have a seizure and she finds somewhere safe to lie down until it's over.

"Valerie stays with her until she comes round, but she didn't come round and the poor dog must have rushed out, looking for help. Thank you, Fran."

"I didn't do anything," she said.

"Clearly you did," he said. "She must have been desperate to get someone to follow her and luckily she found you."

Fran bent down and stroked Valerie's head.

"Clever girl," she said.

"Can I get you a coffee?" Matt asked. "You've had a bit of a shock. The park café is just over the road.

"I won't invite you round to mine as it's not a good idea to go home with a stranger."

He smiled, but his eyes were serious.

She was about to refuse, but realised she had nothing to hurry away for.

A coffee would be nice with this kind man and the two lovely dogs. And she was feeling decidedly shaky after all that running.

"Thank you," she said. "I'd love to."

"Good." He grinned.

They were on their second cup of coffee, sitting in the shade outside the café, when Matt's phone rang.

Fran could tell right away that it was good news.

"That was Alice's daughter," he said. "She's conscious and doing well."

He told Valerie, too, and the Staffie jumped up joyfully as if she understood.

Fran held out her arms and Valerie jumped on to her lap.

As she cuddled the dog, she couldn't help feeling that she hadn't saved anyone. It had been Valerie who'd saved her from making a terrible mistake.

Quietly Matt passed her a tissue and she smiled at him through her tears.

"I'm fine," she assured him, and she was, she really was. ■

ALFRED HITCHCOCK directed Cary Grant, Ingrid Bergman and Claude Rains in this tense romantic thriller. Bergman plays Alicia, the American daughter of a convicted Nazi spy, whose notoriety also derives from her moral reputation. Government agent T.R. Devlin (Grant) recruits Alicia to infiltrate a Nazi cell of her father's friends, now based in Brazil after World War II. Her mission is to become close to Alex Sebastian (Rains), with whom – unbeknownst to Devlin – she has a history. Despite being in love with Devlin, Alicia marries Sebastian, putting duty to country before love, and undertakes her dangerous task.

The uncovering of the Nazis' plot, which revolves around materials for an atomic bomb, is all the more resonant because the film was released just a year after the bomb was dropped on Hiroshima and Nagasaki. Hitchcock claimed he was the subject of FBI interest because he had spoken to researchers about the science behind such devices during the development period of the film, while the details of the Manhattan Project were still secret.

The film was an immediate success, taking nearly $5 million in the first year of release. It is now regarded as a classic.

1946
A golden year for the silver screen

CARY GRANT
INGRID BERGMAN
Notorious!
CLAUDE RAINS
Mise en Scène
ALFRED HITCHCOCK
RKO RADIO PICTURES

# Making Music

## by Jean Robinson

I F that man looks at us again with that face on him I shall have words with him, Eve thought as she straightened in the pew.

She was not going to stop Harry playing his mouth organ. It would only upset him and that could cause more of a disturbance than the muted notes he was producing.

He only ever played it quietly in church, as if he sensed it was a sacred place. Other members of the congregation would look round and smile indulgently.

If that objectionable old man couldn't tolerate a young boy with her son's problems in the house of God then he shouldn't be there, Eve told herself resolutely.

The vicar closed the service with a prayer and the congregation moved towards the small seated area at the back of the church where coffee was served.

"I know it disturbs the service, but it keeps him calm." Eve felt the need to explain to Nancy, who was handing round biscuits. "I don't want to cause any trouble, but if I can't bring Harry I won't be able to come myself."

"It's not a problem, honestly," Nancy said, giving her a concerned look. "Everyone understands. He plays it ever so quietly. And we all love Harry."

"Everyone but Ron." Eve sighed.

Nancy was quick to reassure her.

"I don't know much about him, but I'm sure he doesn't mean to be unkind."

Eve went to sit beside Harry, who was quietly observing everything around him.

She ruffled his blond hair and he looked up at her and gave one of his heart-melting smiles.

Conversation buzzed as more people gathered with their cups of coffee and she began to relax. That was until Harry fished in his pocket

and Eve tensed again.

Ron had seated himself directly opposite them and was half listening to Jack, the organist, who was chatting beside him. But Eve could see that his attention was on Harry.

Even as Harry lifted the instrument to his mouth, she saw Ron's brow crease.

Eve took hold of Harry's hand.

"Come on, love," she said as she ushered her son out of the building. She really couldn't face a confrontation today.

Life was stressful enough without having to explain Harry's problems to someone who would never understand that her son needed this one thing that seemed to calm him whenever he was beginning to grow agitated.

Harry looked up at her, frowning.

"Why are we going home early?" he asked, dragging on her arm.

She squeezed his warm little hand.

"Mummy has a headache," she lied.

His little face screwed up as it always did when he didn't understand something.

She hated to see that look of disappointment on his face. Harry always enjoyed watching the people in church and relished the attention that they gave him.

It was one of the few places she felt safe with him, knowing he wouldn't be stared at or considered odd.

She cursed Ron silently under her breath. Why did he have to come along and spoil everything?

As soon as Eve stepped inside the house the tears threatened as she realised again how alone she was. Harry's father had left soon after he was born.

In the six years since then she'd struggled to give her son the best life possible, and most of the time he seemed happy. She had joined various groups and found a level of support.

But none had given her the same feeling of being included and loved as the small village church.

They had been going for a couple of years now. Harry loved the place, with its beautiful old stained-glass windows and carved wooden pews. He seemed calmer there.

He always knew when it was Sunday and kept a check on the time so they wouldn't be late.

Just hearing the church bells echoing round the village on a crisp spring morning as she and Harry walked the short distance from their home brought joy to Eve's heart.

One day Nancy had taken Harry up into the bell tower and let him pull one of the ropes. He'd talked about it for days afterwards.

Then, six weeks ago, this man had appeared. She had no idea who he was or where he'd come from. Nobody else did, either, as far as she knew. He only ever spoke to a couple of the men.

But whenever Harry brought out his mouth organ he would turn and look at him with a frown on his face.

Nobody else bothered about Harry's unusual behaviour. They accepted him for the loveable little boy he was and had taken him to their hearts, talking to him, making sure he had the chocolate biscuits he loved so much at coffee time.

Her phone rang. It was Jen.

"I just wanted to make sure you're all right, dear. I thought maybe you were a bit upset with Ron."

Warmth spread through her to think Jen cared that much. But she foreced herself to say what was on her mind.

"To be honest, Jen, I don't think we should come again. Harry is obviously causing a nuisance."

"Oh, Eve, don't say that." Jen sounded shocked. "You must come. We'd miss you and little Harry terribly if you stopped.

"Don't take any notice of Ron. He always looks stern. I think it's just his way. I bet he isn't even aware of it."

"We'll see," Eve said.

As they chatted on, her resolve grew. She had some real friends at church, more than she'd ever had: people who cared about her and Harry, people who would miss them if they weren't there.

She must be strong and try to ignore Ron's disapproving looks. Harry hadn't noticed them so why should they worry her?

It was just that so many years of being on the defensive seemed to have caught up with her, and she didn't have any fight left in her.

\* \* \* \*

When next Sunday came round Eve wondered whether she really could face going to church again.

That awful man would be there and he would give her that look again. She knew she would have to challenge him this time and that was bound to cause bad feeling.

Yet she so wanted to go. It was such a welcoming place to be, surrounded by people who were her friends now, people who understood, people who loved Harry. It was the place where she felt most at peace with herself.

Harry came rushing into the bedroom clutching his new trainers, his face aglow.

"Hurry up, Mum, or we'll be late."

This made her mind up. If Harry could do it, so could she.

"Quickly, then. Get yourself dressed. We only have half an hour to get there."

"Can I wear my new shirt?"

"Of course. It's a very special Sunday today and you have to look especially smart. It's Mothering Sunday."

"I know," he said with a smirk. "Mrs James told us at school. We have to be extra good today."

Eve shook her head and smiled at him indulgently.

"You're always a good boy," she told him.

Mothering Sunday. There would be families there, and lots of children. Noisy children would make it easier. Surely today Ron would be more forgiving.

Or maybe he wouldn't be there at all if he disliked children as much as he appeared to.

Eve straightened as she always did when things got tough.

I will go, she told herself. I will not deny my son this pleasure because of some grumpy old man.

\* \* \* \*

Ron was the first person she set eyes on as she entered the building. He was sitting in a pew just ahead of where she always sat.

Eve liked to keep to the same place as Harry didn't cope well with change.

There were nine children amongst the congregation. Ron turned to look at each child in turn. They were all behaving impeccably.

All went quiet as the vicar began with his usual welcome. Harry was calm today so Eve had hopes of a peaceful time. And it was. Harry didn't make a sound.

That was, until the vicar began to pray. Harry took his mouth organ from his pocket. Eve tensed.

# Happy Retirement

I've been retired about a year and goodness, it's all go;
My days are just so active with me rushing to and fro.
I've joined a Sunday Rambling Club, they're such a friendly bunch,
And some of us meet in mid-week; we walk, and then we lunch!
I'm on the cleaning rota for our little village church
And help out if the flower arrangers leave them in the lurch.
I'm hooked by family history – great-grandma was a cop! –
And twice a week I sort donations in the hospice shop.
I help some children with their reading at our lovely school
And on Wednesdays I do aerobics in the swimming pool.
My diary is chock-a-block, it's lovely being busy,
But goodness, all this rushing sometimes leaves me in a tizzy.
I've thought of a solution, and I think it's for the best;
Next week I'm going back to work to have a little rest!

Ewan Smith.

The other children turned as the gentle notes resonated through the ancient church.

It seemed almost to accompany the prayer rather than disrupt it. The vicar glanced at Harry and gave him an indulgent smile as he always did. Ron turned, too. His look was not indulgent.

The vicar involved the children in the service. They answered his questions and listened to his stories. Harry sat, calm now, his expression inscrutable.

Nancy moved to the front of the church holding a basket of flowers and invited the children to come up. Each child was given a small posy of primroses to present to their mothers.

Little Janie took Harry's hand and led him up to the front to collect his posy. He looked pleased.

At coffee time Eve took Harry to sit beside Fran, who always liked to talk to him. Sometimes he responded. Often he just stared at her, but Fran didn't mind. She understood.

Ron positioned himself exactly opposite them as he always did. Harry began to fidget, which was a sign he was uneasy. He took out his mouth organ and quietly began to play one of his favourite tunes.

Eve watched, ready for a fight. Surely nobody could complain about a child playing a mouth organ at coffee time.

It wasn't disturbing anyone. It was hardly noticeable amidst the bright,

lively chatter.

In fact, the chatter often stopped because most of them wanted to listen and encourage Harry.

Eve straightened in her seat. Today she felt she had the courage. If that man gave her son that look again, she would definitely challenge him.

As the music reached him, Ron turned from talking to Jack and gave Harry that look.

When he stood up, Eve tried to get to her feet, determined to confront him.

But suddenly her courage deserted her under his glowering face. Her legs had turned to jelly and she sank back on to her chair. She was no match for a man like Ron.

He moved towards her. Eve was conscious that Jen was now hovering beside her, a concerned expression on her face, and she was grateful for the support.

There was an atmosphere of tension in the room which caused the chatter to fade and dwindle.

"I have been observing your son over the past weeks," Ron began in his brusque voice.

He paused.

Eve took a deep breath.

"I'm sorry for the disturbance Harry causes," she said, "but . . ."

Ron looked surprised.

"Oh, that's not at all the case. I don't find it disturbing in the slightest. I can see your son takes great comfort from his music."

Eve stared up at him, stunned. Ron's face looked serious.

"You're not annoyed with him?" she managed in a husky voice. This had quite taken the wind out of her sails.

"Quite the contrary!" Ron assured her with a slight smile. "In fact, I've rarely seen one so young get such music out of what is in fact a child's toy. It's quite exceptional."

Eve was silent for a moment or two while she processed what Ron was saying.

"You mean – you think he has talent?" she asked at last.

"I do," Ron said emphatically. "It's Eve, isn't it?"

He looked down at the little boy.

"And Harry, I believe. Let me explain. My wife and I lead a group of young musicians. Perhaps you could bring the young fellow along to our practice session next week. We have a selection of musical instruments.

"He could try some and we can see which he might be best suited to. You will, of course, be welcome to stay and listen.

"Most of our mothers do. We usually have tea and biscuits afterwards. It's really quite jolly." Ron's face looked quite kindly now.

"You mean you think he could learn to play a proper instrument?" Eve ventured.

"Certainly." Ron sat down beside her. "That lad's a born musician, you can tell. He ought to be encouraged.

"And I've seen what music can do for these young people. It gives them confidence."

Eve could hardly believe what she was hearing. And he was still giving her that look – the one she'd been misinterpreting all along.

She recognised now that it was a keen look, a look of interest and consideration.

Surprisingly, Harry had been following the conversation and seemed quite at ease with Ron.

He tugged at her sleeve.

"Can I, Mum?"

Eve looked down at her son, saw the light in his eyes and felt herself welling up. People were smiling at her. Jen was nodding her encouragement.

Fran reached across and gave her hand a reassuring squeeze.

She looked up at Ron and managed a grateful smile. Then, with a shaky hand, she scribbled down the details of where this group met.

Leaving the church, she took Harry's hand as he skipped along beside her, chattering excitedly, and Eve felt her heart soaring as happy tears filled her eyes.

She was so glad she hadn't let her preconceptions keep her away from the church that meant so much to them both.

This was indeed a place where miracles happened. ■

*Illustration by Gerard Fay.*

# Last Days Of Summer

## by Glenda Young

SANDRA stood beside the trailer door and waited as her six donkeys walked down the ramp one by one, heading to the golden sands.

She lifted her face to the sun, grateful for the warmth and brightness on such a special day. It was the last day of the season for the donkey rides on the beach, and this last day was always a bittersweet one.

For as much as Sandra enjoyed her life at the farm with husband Dan and their horses, chickens and cows, her time working on the beach each summer with the donkeys was the season she always enjoyed the most.

Knowing that today was the last day of donkey rides that year made Sandra feel wistful. And there was another feeling, something she couldn't quite place.

"Morning, Sandra!" a voice called.

She turned and saw the short, stout figure of Molly Atkins walking

61

towards her.

Molly ran a rock shop on the beach.

"You feeling all right this morning, Sandra?" Molly asked as she drew close. "You're looking a bit peaky."

Sandra pushed her hair from her brow as the breeze whipped around her.

"I'm all right." She smiled. "Guess I'm just upset about it being the last day of the season for the donkeys."

Molly eyed Sandra keenly.

"Looks to me like you could do with some rest," Molly said. "Maybe it's just as well it's the last day.

"Are you and Dan settling the donkeys into the farm over winter as usual?"

Sandra nodded.

"As always, Molly. It'll be good to have them home."

"It does them good being on the beach with people, too," Molly said. She pointed to the donkeys huddled in a group on the beach where two small children, a girl and a boy holding hands, were gaping in awe at the animals.

"Look, you can see how content they are around children."

"I'd better go and get started," Sandra said.

"What time are you planning to leave today?" Molly asked.

"A bit earlier than usual, if I can," Sandra replied. "I've a lot to do on the farm."

Molly nodded.

"Then I'll say my goodbyes now. Once the donkeys are resting at the farm I daresay we won't see you here until spring."

$*$    $*$    $*$    $*$

"How much are your donkey rides?" the little girl asked as Sandra approached.

"Three pounds each," Sandra replied.

There were no adults with the children as far as Sandra could see. She looked at the two of them carefully.

"Are you here on your own?" she asked.

The little boy, shorter and younger looking than the girl, nodded his head.

"Where are your parents?" Sandra asked.

The little girl pointed behind her without even looking in the direction she was indicating.

"Over there," she said.

"No, they're not," the boy said, then he shot the girl a look. "You told a lie."

"It's not a lie, Ben."

"It is, Alice. It is a lie."

He looked Sandra straight in the eye.

"We ran away," he said.

Sandra scanned the beach, desperately trying to find someone who looked as if they were searching for two small children, but try as she might, she couldn't see anyone there.

It was still early. The shops were just opening and business at the beach hadn't yet begun.

In fact, the beach was pretty much empty apart from a couple of locals walking their dogs.

Sandra eyed the two children keenly as they stared up at her, waiting for her to speak.

She glanced over at her donkeys and they, too, were staring, all six pairs of eyes and six tails blowing in the breeze.

Sandra's heart sank.

The last thing she needed was to be saddled with two lost children, today of all days, but she could hardly abandon them.

She glanced around again to see if she could spot any adults who might be looking for Ben and Alice, trying to quell her mounting unease. The truth was, Sandra didn't have very much experience in looking after children.

She saw her sister's daughter just a couple of times a year as they lived so far away.

She spent little time with other people's children and wasn't at all sure what to do with the two standing in front of her now.

Ben and Alice were still holding hands, waiting for her to tell them what to do. Just then, Sandra spotted Molly's husband, Bob, walking along the prom.

"Bob!" she called. "Have you got a minute, please?"

Bob eased himself down the steps to the sands.

"Bob, this is Ben and Alice," Sandra explained. "And they're a little bit lost."

"We're not lost, we've run away," Ben piped up.

Sandra rolled her eyes at Bob and he smiled.

"Well, my guess is that your mum and dad are going to be very worried about you," he said kindly.

"Tell you what — why don't you stay here and give Sandra a bit of a hand with the donkeys and I'll go and see if I can find out where your parents might be?"

"How would you two like to help me set up the donkey rides today?" Sandra asked, delighted that someone else had taken charge.

"Yes, please!" Ben cried. He was so excited that he started jumping up and down on the sand.

"What do we have to do?" Alice said more cautiously. She grabbed Ben's hand and pulled him towards her.

"All we have to do is carry some plastic pails from the trailer to the beach. Do you think you could both help me with that?

"They're not heavy and it's a very important job — the donkeys need them to drink water from."

"I can carry pails!" Ben cried.

"Will you be paying us?" Alice asked.

Sandra laughed.

"Well, let's see – you can have a free donkey ride, how does that sound?"

Ben punched the air in delight while Alice stood still, watching Sandra but not speaking.

"Did you really run away?" Sandra asked the children.

Ben looked at Alice as if waiting for her to speak on behalf of them both.

Alice cast her gaze down, shuffled her trainers against the sand and sniffed back a tear. She nodded her head, unable to speak.

Sandra rummaged in her pocket, brought out a packet of tissues and handed one to the girl.

"Come on, you two. You can give me a hand with the pails and Bob can go and get some help. We'll find your mum and dad for you, just you wait and see."

The children looked at each other.

"She's not our mum," Ben said, shaking his head. "She just married our dad. Our real mum died."

"And we miss her, and we want her back," Alice said. "That's why we ran away."

Bob spoke to Sandra.

"I'll go and let Jim at the tourist office know you've got two young children here, in case anyone is looking for them."

"What's your last name?" Sandra asked.

There was a silence and neither Ben nor Alice spoke.

"Come on, now, you must have a last name," Sandra said. "It will help us to find your . . . your dad."

Alice kicked at the sand with her trainer and wiped the back of her hand across her eyes.

"It used to be Mitchell."

"But it's Mitchell-Sykes now, since Dad's wedding," Ben said.

Bob gave a little cough.

"I'll go and report the children are safe and with you."

Sandra nodded at him and smiled at the children in front of her.

"OK, you two. I think we were just about to go and fetch the donkeys' pails from the van, weren't we?"

Sandra and Bob headed to the trailer with the children following behind.

"I'll report the lost children to the police, too," Bob whispered to Sandra.

"Thanks, Bob," she said. "I'll keep them amused in the meantime."

As Bob hurried off, Sandra and the children carried the pails to where the donkeys were patiently waiting.

Then she showed Alice and Ben how to fill the pails from bottles of water she brought from the trailer.

Once the donkeys had taken a drink, Sandra set up her brightly coloured board advertising rides along the beach.

It was still early in the day and there was no sign of anyone wanting a donkey ride yet.

## All Aboard

I am waiting by the quayside
In a highly nervous state.
I've never been to sea before,
Who knows what lies in wait?
What if we should meet icebergs,
Or the captain lose his way?
And pirates, wrecks and mutiny
Must happen every day.
What if we get scurvy,
Or a tempest starts to blow?
What if there's a giant squid
To drag us down below?
And so my natural doubts and fears
I'm sure you will excuse,
Yet still my friends assure me
I'll enjoy this harbour cruise!

Maggie Ingall.

"Would you two like your free ride on the donkeys now, while it's quiet?" she said.

Alice and Ben nodded enthusiastically.

Sandra lifted Ben on to Spike. He was her favourite donkey, a very calm and gentle soul.

Then she lifted Alice on to an older donkey, Barney.

The donkeys knew exactly what they needed to do once they felt the child's weight on their back.

Sandra simply set off walking the short distance from the beach steps to the cabin where deckchairs could be rented, and the donkeys followed – all six of them.

They walked together or not at all, and it always made Sandra smile to see how they enjoyed being together.

They were the same at the farm, always in a group, as if looking after each other.

When Sandra reached the deckchair cabin, she turned and the donkeys followed. Alice and Ben were giggling, making each other laugh, as the donkeys walked.

Sandra was glad to see she'd been able to put a smile on their faces. She just hoped Bob would be able to get someone down to the beach to help reunite the children with their parents soon.

There was clearly some sort of family problem that the children were having with their new mum, but Sandra knew it wasn't her place to get involved.

Sandra and the donkeys walked to and from the steps to the deckchair

iStock.

65

cabin a couple of times before she told Alice and Ben the donkeys needed to rest.

She was just about to lift the children down on to the sand when a man came running towards them, waving his sunhat in the air and shouting.

"Alice! Ben!"

They turned quickly at the sound of the voice.

"It's Dad!" Alice cried happily.

When the man reached Sandra he pulled Alice and Ben from the donkeys and swept them up in his arms.

"Thank you," he said to Sandra. "I've been frantic, searching for them everywhere."

He put Alice and Ben on the sand and sank to his knees in front of them, holding tight to their hands.

"Why did you run away? What's wrong?"

Alice and Ben glanced at Sandra.

"You need to tell your dad what you told me before," she said gently.

Sandra left the family to their discussion. She guessed the children were struggling to cope with major changes to their lives.

Out on the sands Sandra saw a woman in a white dress walking towards them.

The three of them stood to greet the woman. Sandra watched as Alice shyly took hold of one of the woman's hands and Ben took the other before the foursome walked away.

Sandra hoped the little family would manage to work things out. She had been surprised to find that she had enjoyed her short time with Ben and Alice.

She certainly hadn't had much experience with children, but she thought she'd done OK, for a novice.

She turned her attention back to the donkeys.

She patted Spike's neck as she cast her mind back over the summer months, trying to work out how exactly many weeks she and the donkeys had been working at the beach, with the early starts and long afternoons walking up and down.

And she remembered how hard she and Dan had been working at the farm, too.

No wonder she'd been so tired lately!

But this was the last day, and sorry as she would be to say goodbye to the sand and sea for another year, she was looking forward to a rest.

Still, something was niggling at the back of her mind.

As she counted the weeks and recalled the summer months, it struck her.

Slowly, Sandra put her hand to her stomach as the truth dawned on her. Then she turned her face to the sun and smiled.

She breathed deeply, savouring the smell and sounds of the ocean, for she knew she would remember this day.

Her life on the beach for the year was ending, but a new one was just beginning. ■

# Plockton

Plockton on the shores of Loch Carron is known as the Jewel of the Highlands, attracting many visitors to its stunning waterside setting with hills encasing it. It is well linked by road and rail, attracting plenty of visitors to the area, with photographers and artists keen to capture its beauty.

The tiny harbour is dotted with a line of quaint cottages, with yachts and palm trees adding to the idyllic scene. Seal-spotting and fishing trips are popular pastimes and bikes are available to rent if you want to explore the area on two wheels. Among the wildlife to be seen are otters, red squirrel and deer.

Just one kilometre east of Plockton is Duncraig Castle, set in beautiful wooded grounds. The grand mansion was built in 1866 for Alexander Matheson, an MP and businessman. In its time it has served as a military hospital during World War II and a boarding school, finally becoming a luxurious B&B. Eileen Donan Castle is a little more than six miles from Plockton – it's well worth a visit.

# Lorna's Legacy

## by Vanda Inman

**E**XCUSE me, have you lost a pair of socks?"

Molly turned to find a woman standing behind her holding a pair of blue and white striped socks with lions on them.

"Oh, yes." Molly laughed and gestured towards the buggy she was pushing. "That's the third time he's thrown them out this morning."

She put the socks back on Jake's feet and he promptly dropped his sunhat on to the pavement.

"Beautiful flowers," Molly continued, noticing the trowel in the woman's hand. "Do you look after them?"

The long border beside the bowling club was filled with bright cottage garden flowers, lupins, cornflowers, pansies and poppies, a colourful array of pink, purple, blue and yellow.

The woman smiled and held out her hand.

"I'm Lorna, and thank you. When I started it was all brambles."

She paused, bright blue eyes shining with the memory.

"It was a challenge but I'm happy with it now. They're all plants to attract insects and birds. It belongs to the bowling club, but a few years ago I seemed to be at a loose end so I asked if I could look after it.

"People said I was mad, because it wasn't mine, but you don't need to own something to care, and it's brought its own rewards. So many people stop to admire the flowers and have a chat."

Lorna peeped beneath the hood of the buggy.

"Is this your grandson? He's gorgeous."

Molly laughed.

"We've already lost his sunhat twice this morning," she replied. A loud giggle came from the buggy when Lorna tickled Jake under his chin.

"My daughter-in-law's expecting in a couple of months." Lorna looked enthusiastic, then wistful. "But they live in Scotland so I'm not sure how often I'll get to see the new arrival, living down here in Cornwall."

*Illustration by iStock.*

She turned back to the border.

"I need to move this buddleia; it isn't happy here at all. It needs to be in the sun, but uprooting is always difficult. Anyway, enjoy your grandson, and do take any seeds for your own garden when the time comes."

\* \* \* \*

Molly manoeuvred the buggy into the hallway of the tiny flat and, after some jiggling, managed to get it into the living-room and find a space.

"How was he?" Sarah asked as she took Jake out of the buggy and popped him into the playpen.

"Ever so good, except for trying to lose his socks and hat. I was a while talking to the lady who looks after that great long border up by the bowling club and he didn't make a fuss at all.

"She said how gorgeous he is and asked if he was my grandson."

"As good as," Sarah replied.

"Anything else you'd like me to do?" Molly asked, but Sarah shook her head.

"You sit down and I'll make us both a cuppa. Kettle's just boiled."

Sarah returned with two mugs of tea and set them down with a troubled look on her face.

"What's up?" Molly asked at once.

"I don't know how to tell you this," she began, "but we're going to have to move. This flat is too small now, and although the location is perfect, we need to find a different area to afford to rent a larger house."

She looked sad.

"I'm afraid there's no other option."

\* \* \* \*

Later that evening Molly thought about Lorna. She hadn't corrected her when she'd asked if Jake was her grandson and they'd gone on to talk about other things, but the truth was that Sarah, her husband Ben and Jake were no relation at all.

They lived in a ground-floor flat across the road from Molly, who lived in the Victorian house she'd grown up in.

She'd never married and, having retired, had plenty of time on her hands. She would have liked to have a family of her own but things didn't always work out as planned, and Molly was happy enough.

When Jake was a baby, Molly had occasionally helped Sarah by taking him for a stroll in his pram while she had a rest.

Then, when Sarah went back to work part-time, Molly began looking after Jake one day a week. She delivered and collected him from nursery on another and fitted in a bit of housework here and there.

It was an arrangement which Molly loved, though her friend, Freda, wasn't impressed.

"You spend too much time running around after that family," she often commented. "We never seem to go out for coffee any more, and when was the last time you called round to watch the telly with me of an evening?

"Too tired, I expect, that's the truth of it. Think how much easier life would be if I moved in with you as a lodger.

"It would save us both money, we'd be company for each other and you wouldn't need to be running around after other people all the time."

Molly had to admit that her babysitting duties had taken up a lot of her time, but how could she say that she enjoyed looking after little Jake more than spending time with Freda?

And, although Freda often mentioned becoming her lodger, Molly wasn't entirely sure it would be a good idea.

Freda had a habit of liking things her own way.

"How about coming for a walk with us tomorrow afternoon?" Molly invited in desperation, but Freda grumbled that she had better things to do, although Molly was at a loss to know what.

It was when Molly was pottering in her rather overgrown garden that the idea came to her.

Lorna had said that something didn't need to belong to you for you to look after it. Molly paused.

The little family didn't belong to her at all but that didn't mean she couldn't care for them. Help and feelings weren't only restricted to family members or what someone owned.

She had a four-bedroomed house with a large garden, and Sarah and her family were desperate for more space.

Molly had thought of moving to somewhere smaller but didn't want to uproot herself from her childhood home.

Why not invite Sarah and her family to move in? It could solve all their problems.

Should she? Could she?

"Utterly ridiculous," Freda announced at once, making Molly regret she'd brought the subject up. But she needed to bounce the idea off someone and Freda was the only person around.

"Give away your home? To people you barely know and spend most of your life skivvying for? Whatever next?

"You'd be nothing but a live-in housemaid. You wouldn't catch me doing it." She stirred her coffee vigorously. "Much better you have me to come and live with you. We'd have a nice peaceful time together."

"I'm not giving anything away," Molly retorted. "I'm only suggesting we split my house into two, which can be done quite easily, and they rent the larger part.

"I'd still have my own space and they'd have plenty of room. Ben would look after the garden, which would be great for little Jake, and I wouldn't have to uproot myself."

Freda snorted, but the more Molly thought about it the better the idea became. She thought of Lorna, wishing she could talk to her about it.

She'd only met her once and, although she often walked that way, hadn't bumped into her again. But something about her gentle presence and optimistic outlook on life had made an impression.

*    *    *    *

The next few months were busy and it was autumn before Molly returned to the border at the bowling club to collect the seeds Lorna had offered.

She wanted to tell her what had happened and hear all about Lorna's own grandchild, which should have arrived by now, because the idea of renting part of the house had been a resounding success.

"Are you really sure?" Ben had asked. "We'll be the best tenants ever and look after it all for you. It would be a life-saver for us.

"One of the reasons Sarah's reluctant to move is because you've become such a part of our lives."

Molly smiled, thinking that it was she who was getting the better part of the deal. Less worry about the house and garden and, after all these years, some fun and laughter around the place.

She was sorry Freda had been upset with the idea, but sharing with her simply wouldn't have worked.

When Molly arrived at the bowling club Lorna wasn't there, but a man was busy hoeing the border.

She was about to speak but a sign on the fence caught her eye and she stopped short. *Lorna's Legacy.*

"Oh!" Molly's hand flew to her mouth.

The man turned, and she found herself looking into a pair of bright blue eyes exactly like Lorna's.

"I'm so sorry," Molly said, "but I've just seen the sign. I haven't been here for months and was hoping to catch her . . ."

The man smiled apologetically.

"I've only just put the sign up because people were always asking after her and wanted to remember all the work she did here – and the words of wisdom she gave."

He held out a hand.

"I'm Paul, Lorna's brother."

"Molly." She paused. "I only met Lorna once but she was such a lovely woman. Our meeting changed my life for the better. She said I could come and collect seeds any time I wanted, and . . ."

"Help yourself," Paul offered. "When did you see Lorna?"

"In May," Molly replied. "She told me her son and his wife were expecting a baby in a couple of months."

She paused and surveyed the border, the bright yellows, pinks and blues of May now faded to rich autumnal tones of red and orange.

## New Kitten

I missed my old and much-loved cat, her loss was such a blow,
But, seventeen, and very frail, it was her time to go.
That's it! I said, there'll be no more, this is a pet-free zone,
But conscious of the empty house, I really felt alone.

And then I heard about a friend, who must rehome a kitten,
You could just look, the family said – I looked, and I was smitten!
He really was the cutest thing, all black with four white paws,
His eyes were huge and round and bright, and oh! his needle claws!

So now he has a brand-new home, and he is just spoiled rotten,
My days of feeling all alone are simply quite forgotten.
His kitten antics make me laugh through fair and stormy weather,
And now it is my greatest wish that we'll grow old together!

Eileen Hay.

"I'd like to help," she said suddenly.

"Great," Paul replied. "There's a little group of us taking over what Lorna used to do single-handed. A bit of autumn pruning's in order."

He grinned.

"Meet you here on Friday, ten a.m. sharp."

*   *   *   *

The following Friday, Molly arrived, gardening gloves and secateurs in hand. Talking to Paul had brought back so many memories of that day in May when she'd met Lorna.

Jake was walking now, running around most of the time and still intent on taking off his socks and losing his hat if he could.

"I told Lorna you were coming today and she remembered you," Paul announced when Molly arrived. "She wanted to know how your grandson is and to tell you she's having a wonderful time with hers."

Molly gasped. How could Paul possibly have spoken to her?

"I thought Lorna . . ." Molly's gaze wandered to the sign.

"She moved to Scotland," Paul said, smiling. "To be with her new grandson. Uprooting was hard, but she decided that was her place. And it was talking to you that helped her make the decision.

"Are you OK?" He took her arm. "Come to the café for a cup of coffee."

"So she's OK?" Molly asked, relief sweeping through her.

"Fit as a fiddle and sorting out their garden," Paul replied with a grin. "Seeing you with your grandson definitely helped her realise where she should be. She's absolutely flourishing now."

"He isn't actually my grandson," Molly admitted, "but that's a long story. Suffice to say Lorna had a great effect on my life, too. Strange, isn't it? And we only met once."

\* \* \* \*

"About time, too," Freda grumbled when Molly invited her out a few weeks later. "Where shall we go?"

"It's a surprise," Molly replied. "But bring your gardening gloves."

When they arrived at the bowling club café she introduced Paul to Freda.

"We're both going to help the gardening group weed the border outside. It's a lovely sunny afternoon and will do us good," she added sternly as Freda opened her mouth to object.

An hour later, Molly looked at her watch. It was time to pick Jake up from nursery, but she had no worries about Freda now.

She and Paul had been deep in conversation, and Freda had been chatting to other members of the group, too. She'd even noticed a tinkling, almost girlish laugh from Freda, something she hadn't heard in a long while.

"See you later, I'm off," Molly called, and they all waved.

There was only just one very small thing. Molly sighed.

She had so liked Paul and enjoyed their conversations before she'd brought Freda along, but it looked as though Freda might be the one to win his heart now.

She shook herself sternly. She had nothing to complain about.

Everything had worked out perfectly and Sarah was expecting again, so there would be another baby to push around, and more socks and hats to lose. Molly would have plenty to do, especially if she continued helping the gardening group.

"Molly, wait."

She turned to see Paul hurrying to catch up with her, pulling off his gloves as he did so.

"I know you're going to pick up Jake, but might I walk with you, and maybe take you out for a cup of tea afterwards?"

"But Freda . . ." Molly couldn't help wondering what she would think, but Paul laughed.

"She's fine," he replied, gesturing towards Freda laughing with another member of the group.

"In that case, thank you," Molly replied.

It occurred to her that suddenly she had everything she'd ever wanted in life: a family to care for and now someone to care for her.

And as Paul linked his arm with hers she thought fleetingly that, wherever Lorna was in the world, her legacy and her way of helping people lived on. ▪

JOHN FORD directed this retelling of the famous 1881 gunfight at the OK Corral, the culmination of the feud between the Earp and Clanton families in Tombstone, Arizona.

Henry Fonda plays Wyatt Earp, Victor Mature is Doc Holliday and Cathy Downs is the eponymous Clementine Carter.

The film is roughly based on a biography of Wyatt Earp, though Clementine herself is not a historical character. It tells of events leading up to the real 30-second gunfight between lawman Earp and his posse, and the Clanton-McLaury gang of lawbreaking cowboys from a nearby ranch.

Not long after the murder of Earp's brother, Clementine arrives in town to find Doc Holliday, an old flame. He's involved with another girl and tells her to leave. When she refuses, Doc leaves.

His new girl fights with Clementine, and inadvertently reveals a clue for Wyatt about the murder. The popular ballad "Oh, My Darling Clementine" is heard at the beginning and end of the film.

It was one of the top-grossing films in 1946 and has enjoyed critical acclaim ever since, with many critics and viewers declaring this to be "the perfect Western".

1946
A golden year for the silver screen

Darryl F. Zanuck
presents
JOHN FORD'S
MY DARLING CLEMENTINE

HENRY FONDA · LINDA DARNELL · VICTOR MATURE

WALTER BRENNAN
TIM HOLT
CATHY DOWNS

DIRECTED BY
JOHN FORD

PRODUCED BY
SAMUEL G. ENGEL

# The Life Of Riley

## by Teresa Ashby

ILEY took one look at the small ferryboat bobbing up and down on the choppy grey water and threw his arms round Alan. He'd never been so frightened in all his five and a bit years and his stomach churned like the washing in Mum's new front loader.

"What is it?" his stepfather said, bewildered. "You're not scared, are you? Look, you can see the other side. We won't be on the boat for very long."

"Noooo!" Riley wailed. "I don't want to go on the boat. I want to go home."

The big town on the other side of the river had everything their small town did not. There were cinemas and swimming pools, and a big funfair that had set up for the summer.

"Can't we go by train?" Riley pleaded.

"It would take us half a day to get there," Alan replied. "We'd miss the start of the film. You've been looking forward to seeing the 'Robin Hood' cartoon ever since we saw it on 'Disney Time'."

Riley released his grip on Alan and took a step back, cuffing at his soaked face with his sleeve.

"I want to go home," he said.

"But you were looking forward to going for your first ride on the ferry."

Riley's mouth opened, but no words came out, just a torrent of sobs and anguished howls.

Alan looked around, embarrassed.

"Are you coming aboard or not?" the grizzled old ferryman demanded. "I've got a schedule to keep."

"No!" Riley cried.

"All right, all right," Alan said. "We'll go home, but you're being silly. That ferry has been going back and forth across the river for donkey's years and no-one's ever drowned yet."

*Illustration by Gerard Fay.*

They'd moved into Alan's house in the village after Riley's mum married him a few months before. Alan had often mentioned a trip across the river and Riley had been quite keen until he saw the froth on top of the waves.

Riley's eyes stung from crying as he trotted to keep up with Alan. He wished Alan had moved into their flat instead of them having to move to his house when he and Riley's mum got married.

Where they used to live, they didn't have to go on a boat if they wanted to go to the cinema. And yet here they were, far away from all his friends and family.

"Why are you back?" Sandra said. "Is the ferry not running today?"

"Ask him," Alan growled. "I try to do something nice for the boy and he ends up making a huge fuss in front of everyone. I felt such a fool. I wish I hadn't bothered."

He stormed out and moments later they heard the putt-putt-putt of his scooter disappearing down the road.

Sandra turned to look at Riley.

"What happened?"

"I didn't want to go on the boat," Riley blurted out. "It was scary. I didn't mean to make Alan cross."

"I know." She pulled him to her and wrapped her arms round him. "Alan's trying really hard to be a good dad. He's new to all this and he's not always going to get it right, but he'll learn.

"We just have to give him time."

"Why did we have to move here?" Riley sobbed. "I miss home. I miss my friends."

"I know, sweetheart, and that's why Alan wanted you to have a fun day out." She sat down and pulled Riley on to her lap, smoothing his hair from his wet face.

"I'm sure Alan will come round. He was really looking forward to seeing the new Disney film with you."

That made Riley feel worse. He rested his face against his mum's shoulder and the tears kept falling until her blouse was soaked.

He didn't remember the first time his mum brought Alan home, but he could remember how life had changed.

For the first time in his life, he got to ride on someone's shoulders, way up high, and he'd clung on to clumps of Alan's long curly hair.

Alan had laughed.

"Steady on there, mate. I don't want to end up looking like Yul Brynner!"

Alan had even taken him for a ride on the back of his Lambretta, which had been fun. He'd been best man at Mum and Alan's wedding and had been trusted to look after the ring even though he was only five.

And now he'd ruined everything.

The only sound in the kitchen was the clock on the wall ticking, but then the Lambretta came back.

Sandra tightened her arms around him as Alan walked in.

"Put this on, Riley," he said, handing over a small crash helmet. "If we can't go by boat, I'll take you to a closer cinema on the back of my scooter."

"You can't!" Sandra protested. "It's dangerous. He's only little! What if he falls off?"

Riley pulled the helmet on and grinned at Alan.

"He won't fall off," Alan said. "And I'll drive carefully, I promise. When I get back I'll be arranging driving lessons. Now I have a family, I should get a car. Do you think that's a good idea, Riley?"

"Yes, Dad," Riley said, and it was Sandra and Alan who ended up in tears.

\*     \*     \*     \*

On the radio, Queen sang about breaking free and Riley wished he could. For two pins, he'd burst out of the house and take off down the road, never to be seen again.

But then Alan would be disappointed.

"You'll be fine," Alan said as he brushed cat fur off the shoulders of Riley's new suit. "I'm proud of you, son. Very proud."

"I'm just going to be a runner, Dad," Riley said.

"Everyone has to start somewhere," Alan said. "Runners go on to be clerks and managers and you never know where it might lead."

Alan had always had great belief in Riley's abilities.

"I'd better go," Riley said, picking up the briefcase Alan had bought him. He was going to feel daft going to work carrying that, as if he was someone important. All it had in it was his sandwiches.

When he'd gone to the big town across the water for his interview, Alan had insisted on driving him all the way round, but now he was a daily commuter, he'd have to go on the ferry like everyone else.

Every day. There and back.

He'd managed to avoid going on the ferryboat all his life, but now he had no choice.

Alan shook his hand, then turned it into a hug.

"Want me to come and wave you off?"

"No!" Riley said quickly. "I'll see you later, Dad."

He left the house. Some of the neighbours were out enjoying the June sunshine as he walked past.

"Your mum would be so proud of you," Mrs West called out with tears in her eyes.

Riley felt an ache in his chest. He wished she hadn't mentioned Mum. She'd died four years ago and he would never get used to her not being around.

He stopped when he reached the top of the walkway that led down to the pontoon. A dozen people waited for the ferry. It only carried up to twenty passengers and Riley had been hoping there would be twenty people waiting.

The water was flat and silky. It would be a smooth crossing, but the old fear was there, churning round in his stomach.

Everyone else was chatting and laughing and he stood slightly away from the rest, his cheeks blazing. What if he was ill and made a fool of himself?

He tried to work out in his head how long it would take him to pass his driving test so he could drive to work.

The drive took at least an hour both ways rather than fifteen minutes on the ferry, but it would be worth it if he didn't have to contend with this fear every day.

The pontoon began to move beneath his feet and he almost stumbled as the ferry chugged towards them.

"You can do this, Riley." He heard Alan's voice in his head.

Just how disappointed would his stepfather be if he turned up back at home after all the trouble he'd been to? Not only had Alan driven him to his interview, he'd bought him a suit and a briefcase.

He had a horrible thought that it would be the same old ferryman as before and worse, he'd remember Riley making a huge fuss, but it was a young woman who jumped off the boat and tied it up.

"All aboard," she called out. "Hello, Maxine, are you better? Andy! How's your new baby? Hello, John. Morning, Steve. Hello, Trevor."

She greeted every one of the passengers by name as they boarded and hesitated when Riley stepped forward.

"You're new," she said and he noticed that her eyes were as blue as the river. "I'm Steph."

He knew her from school, but had never seen her close up before.

"Riley," Riley said, his voice croaky.

"Of course," she said. "I know you. You were in the same year as me at school. We used to go in on the same bus."

He reddened.

"You always sat upstairs at the front," he recalled.

"And you always sat downstairs at the back."

A familiar grizzled face looked out of the wheelhouse.

"When you've done chatting up my customers, we have a schedule to keep!"

"All right, Grandpa, don't get your whiskers in a knot." Steph laughed. "Will you be travelling all week? We do a discount if you book the week in advance."

"Stop flirting and get on with it." One of the older men laughed. "We'll be late for work."

She sorted out his fare and asked where he was working.

"Scout Shipping," he replied.

"Gary works there, don't you, Gary?" Steph said. "As an export clerk. He's quite ferocious, but not as bad as the manager."

"Ferocious?" Gary guffawed.

"I was joking," she said quickly, seeing the look of horror on Riley's face. "It's a nice, family-run company. They called it Scout Shipping after their dog."

"True," Gary said. "Sometimes the boss brings Scout to work with him. Pleased to meet you, Riley."

Everyone else made jumping aboard the boat look easy, but Riley clung to the rail and stepped from the bobbing pontoon to the bobbing boat, worrying what on earth it was going to be like in bad weather.

He sat down next to Gary, who grinned at him.

"Do you drive?"

Riley shook his head.

"My dad's giving me lessons, but I haven't booked my test yet."

"The ferry doesn't run in really bad weather," Gary went on. "I drive round in that case. I'd be happy to give you a lift.

"You can give me your address later. We'd have to leave a lot earlier, of course."

"I've no problem getting up early. I used to do a paper round."

His face went even redder as a little hum of laughter went round the boat.

Steph's grandpa spun the boat round and headed back across the mouth of the river. Riley prayed he'd be able to hang on to his breakfast, but about halfway across, he realised he was enjoying the experience.

It helped that Steph had come to sit down, too, and her happy chatter took his mind off his fear. Besides, there was something exhilarating about being surrounded by water with the wind in his hair and the sun on his face.

As they approached the docks, the cruise ships, ferries and cargo vessels got bigger and bigger.

He was going to enjoy this.

\*   \*   \*   \*

Riley stood on the quayside with the brisk wind riffling through his hair and the taste of salt on his lips as he looked at home on the other side of the river.

The briefcase Alan had bought for him 13 years ago was packed full of his stuff and he had an envelope in his breast pocket that felt as if it was burning a hole through to his heart.

He watched as Steph brought the ferryboat in and saw she had Megan and Michael with her. Her crew today was Roy, a retired fisherman.

As Riley boarded with the rest of the regulars, Steph kissed his cheek.

"How come he gets special treatment?" Trevor asked. "I've never yet had a kiss just for catching the ferry."

"You never asked me to marry you," Steph retorted with a grin.

There was a real family atmosphere among the ferry commuters. They car-shared if the ferry wasn't running and had supported each other through all sorts over the years, sharing celebrations and commiserations.

But today Riley wasn't ready to share with anyone.

"Daddy!" the kids cried and enveloped him in huge hugs with their little arms.

Usually they were with Steph's mum, Lyn, or Alan, but occasionally, Steph let them ride on the boat for the last trip of the day.

Riley gulped down the lump in his throat and sat with his briefcase between his feet and an arm around each of his children.

He felt like crying. He didn't know what to do.

The boat bounced across the waves while the children giggled with glee. They were as at home on the water as their mother and loved the feeling of salt spray hitting their faces.

It was the last run of the day and as the passengers disembarked, Steph said goodbye to all of them.

"See you tomorrow, Trevor. Goodnight, Steve, give my love to Becky. Have a good evening, Maxine . . ."

She turned to look at Riley and tilted her head to one side. The first time he saw her do that was the moment he fell in love with her all those years ago.

"Something wrong, Riley?" she asked as he helped the children on to the pontoon.

Not that they needed help. They'd been doing this since they could walk.

"Why do you ask?"

"Because you look so sad and worried," she replied.

"Just tired, love," he said.

He had some fanciful notion of finding another job before telling her he'd been made redundant, but knew he would never get away with it. She knew him too well.

"Alan's invited us for dinner tonight," she said. "That OK?"

"Sounds great."

She secured the boat for the night and linked her arm through his as they walked to Alan's house, the children running along ahead.

"Actually, I do have some news," he said, wondering how he could put a positive spin on this. "I've been made redundant. I've got a cheque in my pocket.

"It isn't much, but we'll be all right for a few months. I'll soon get another job. I may even be able to get one this side of the river."

Steph took a deep breath.

"OK," she said. "We should look on this as a new opportunity."

"Exactly," he said.

"There have been a lot of redundancies over the last four or five years," she said. "I've noticed a big drop in the amount of passengers I'm taking back and forth. It's why I've cut the amount of trips I'm doing."

"I know," he said, worried.

It seemed like everything was going wrong for them at once.

"What an amazing stroke of luck," Alan said when Riley told him his news after they'd eaten. "Don't just put the money in the bank and watch it dwindle away. Do something positive with it."

"Like what?" Riley asked.

"Buy another boat."

"Sorry, Alan," Steph said. "That's out of the question. It's not enough to buy a boat, and besides, I've had to cut back on my trips over the river."

"How about trips upriver?" Alan said. "Pleasure trips, birthday parties or even the other way, out into the sea and along the coast. Everyone loves a boat trip.

"If you have a good business plan, I'm sure the bank would give you an advance."

"I don't know the first thing about driving a boat," Riley said.

"You didn't know how to ride a bike or drive a car until I taught you," Alan replied.

* * * *

The sun beat down on the sea, casting sparkles of light across the surface. This trip came with a stop at a beach and a picnic.

It didn't matter how many times he did it, Riley enjoyed it as much as his passengers.

"Everyone ready?" he asked and they all cheered.

He pulled away from the pontoon just as Steph was coming back from the docks on the opposite side on the old ferryboat. She gave him a wave as they passed each other.

Sometimes they swapped and he did the commuter run.

Life would be perfect right now if it wasn't for Alan. Riley's eyes clouded for a moment. His stepfather had recently been diagnosed with cancer and the treatment was harsh, but the doctors were hopeful.

He bit hard on his lip.

The truth was, he'd been avoiding Alan as much as possible, leaving his care to everyone else. He couldn't bear to see his stepfather so ill. He'd never felt so helpless and useless in his life.

He'd even been doing extra river trips.

"Look to your left, ladies and gentlemen," he said. "You may see Muntjac deer running through the trees. The small wooded area is a haven for wildlife, from hedgehogs to woodpeckers."

There was a clatter as people got their binoculars and cameras out.

"I'll take us in a little closer. We have seen badgers and foxes on occasion."

He steered the boat towards the riverbank and cut the engine, giving his passengers plenty of time to look and enjoy the scenery.

He hadn't even known any of this existed until he started doing the trips, and it had been a learning curve. He doubted he would have been here at all if it wasn't for his dad.

Alan had been a rock throughout his life, always there for him no matter what. He owed him so much and he was being an idiot for avoiding him. His mum would be ashamed of him.

Joe, his crew for the day, put a hand on Riley's arm.

"If you want to take some time off, I can get my brother to cover for you."

Riley squeezed his eyes shut.

"Thank you," he whispered.

When his last trip of the day was over, he popped round to Alan's house. Lyn, Steph's mum, was there and she got up to leave when Riley arrived.

She kissed his cheek.

"He'll be so pleased you're here, Riley."

"Hello, son," Alan said, smiling.

He looked thin and grey and his once dark hair was grey and wispy. It broke Riley's heart, but this wasn't about him. It was about Alan.

"Sorry I haven't been around much, Dad," he said.

"I understand. It's good you've been so busy. You have to make hay during the summer, don't you. So, what can I do for you?"

"More to the point, what can I do for you, Dad?" Riley said. "Is there anything you feel like doing? Anywhere you'd like to go?"

"Actually, there is," Alan said. "I'd love a trip out on the boat if you can squeeze me on some time."

"How about I take us all out for a family picnic? Would you be up to that?"

"I'm not on my last legs yet." Alan chuckled.

"I've found this fantastic little beach upriver," Riley said. "It's so peaceful. You could believe you were on a desert island."

"Sounds perfect," Alan said. "Will Michael and Megan bring their latest flames? And you'll ask Lyn along?"

"Oh, yes," Riley said. "Definitely."

"I'll look forward to that, son. It'll do me the world of good. Just what the doctor ordered, eh?"

∗　∗　∗　∗

When he was a small boy, it was just Riley and his mum. Now his family half-filled a boat!

Michael and his wife were sitting in the boat with their three children. Megan and her partner were there with their two and, of course, Steph's mum, Lyn, was handing out sweets and bottles of flavoured water.

"What?" she said when she saw Riley and Steph looking at her. "It's just a little snack."

"We know, Mum." Steph laughed.

"Your grandpa didn't mind you having sweets on the boat, Stephanie," Lyn went on.

Riley remembered Steph's grandpa with great fondness. He'd been the one to convince Steph's parents that they weren't too young to get married. He said it was as obvious as the whiskers on his chin that they were in love.

"Don't let them spoil their appetites," Steph said. "We've packed enough food for an army."

"Not to mention a massive cake," Riley whispered.

They didn't run the river crossing any more. Jobs had dried up over at the port and people tended to drive out to closer big towns for work.

They only had one boat now and Steph still ran the river trips in summer while Riley had had a complete change of career and was now a qualified paramedic.

It was helping to take care of Alan when he was so ill that had decided him. He had no regrets. His job wasn't always easy and could sometimes be heartbreaking, but at last he'd found his niche.

"When are we going?" six-year-old Chloe asked.

"We're just waiting for Great-grandad," Riley said and he felt the faintest frisson of unease.

Where was Alan? He'd been there when they were packing up the picnic, but at some point he'd disappeared.

"Shall I nip round to see if he's at home?" Michael asked.

"I'll go with you," Megan said, but then a shout went up.

"Ahoy! Wait for me!"

Riley looked up and saw Alan at the top of the steps with a huge bottle of champagne in each hand.

"Where have you been, Alan?" Lyn said. "We were getting worried."

"Nagging me already and we've only been married an hour," Alan responded with a grin. "I forgot the champagne, my lovely!"

"Well, in that case, you're forgiven." Lyn smiled.

"Let's get this wedding picnic underway," Steph said. "All aboard!"

"I'll take the helm," Michael said.

"Hey, Dad!" Megan said. "Does this mean that grandad is now our step-grandad and he's your father-in-law as well as your dad?"

Riley laughed as Alan hopped aboard, very spritely for a man of seventy-five who had been at death's door a decade ago.

He and Lyn had become close during his illness, but they'd only just got round to tying the knot.

"Everybody ready?" Michael called out. "Chocks away!"

"That's planes." Steph giggled, rolling her eyes.

As the boat bounced across the waves, everyone on board was laughing and none more than Riley. It had been a good life, he thought, a very good life. And there was still so much more to come. ■

# Nash Point, Glamorgan

The steep cliffs of Nash Point make for a dramatic setting, and at their rugged foot is the beach – home to rock pools and many fossils. Part of the Glamorgan Heritage Coast, the area is perfect for walkers, with lots of trails making the most of the landscape. On a clear day you can see for miles.

Take in the Grade II listed Nash Point Lighthouses – the last to be manned in Wales. The lighthouses were designed by James Walker in direct response to the tragic loss of the *Frolic* after she smashed into a sandbank – more than 55 lives were lost.

Also worth a visit is St Donat's Castle and Arts Centre, once owned by American newspaper magnate Randolph Hearst. Many Hollywood guests are said to have been entertained here. A rare example of a 12th-century castle, it's open to the public on selected days.

Wildlife lovers will also be able to spot a wide variety of birds, from buzzards to peregrine falcons. The lighthouse meadow is a Site of Special Scientific Interest for its notable fauna.

# A Job For Judith

## by Em Barnard

AS under housemaid, one of Judith's jobs was dusting above stairs, and this gave her access to the master's library. She knew she might get caught one day. But if she didn't read and learn she'd never get on in the world.

So her mother was always telling her . . . Oh, dear. It was so hard to say that Mum used to tell her.

Tears began to well again but were blinked away on hearing the master's raised voice in the hall.

Fearing he was heading here, and unable to push the book she held back between its neighbours, she ran with it to behind the door.

When he flung it open, as he did every door in the house, Judith grabbed the knob and tugged it tight to her.

"I've told you before, Lydia," he barked, "you'll marry who I say!"

"I will not, Stepfather."

"Don't use that tone with me or I'll have you married to the marquis tomorrow. Is that understood?"

Judith chanced a peep. The master was hidden by the door, but she could see Miss Lydia standing this side of his desk, hands clenched.

"Is that understood?"

"Clearly!" Lydia snatched up her skirts and flounced round to leave. She spotted Judith and halted in surprise.

Judith's eyes grew wide with fear, for Miss Lydia had only been back here a month, and Judith hadn't spoken more than two words to her.

Lydia swung back.

"By the way, that dog's scrabbling in your roses again."

As her stepfather rushed to the window the two girls made their escape. Lydia led the way, dashing down the hall, flinging the door open to the servants' stairway and running up the spiral stairs.

Along the landing, they made it to Lydia's bedroom unseen.

Lydia leaned against the door and let out a puff of relief.

"Is that book from the library?" she asked.

Illustration by David Young.

Set in 1870

Judith handed it to her with a little curtsey.

"I wasn't stealing it, Miss Lydia. I read a few pages when I lay the fire or dust the room." She straightened the cap perched on her dark hair.

"'Jane Eyre'. That's big reading for an under housemaid."

"I'm twelve. I could say my letters when I was four," Judith said proudly.

"But that's remarkable. Who taught you?" Lydia sat down on her window seat and spread her dress conscientiously.

"Mum served at the railway station café. There were always newspapers left on the tables at the end of the day so she brought them home for me and my sister.

"Mum never had the chance to be educated but she always wanted us to make something of ourselves. Please don't tell I've been reading the books," Judith finished, wiping a tear away.

Lydia patted the window seat.

"Come and sit. I won't tell, so please don't cry. You're Judith, I think." She nodded.

"It's just that my mum died the other week and I miss her."

"I'm so sorry. I lost my mother when I was about your age, so I know what it's like to lose someone you love.

"I was sent to Switzerland to become a lady. That's where I met Oliver. He is a marquis, too, but gentle and kind. And I love him," Lydia added softly, staring out of the window.

"But then I was brought back here. Stepfather wants me to marry that fat Marquis of Walton. He owns the adjoining estate and marriage to me will bring greater wealth and power. But I don't care about that, I want to marry Oliver."

"Would that be the gentleman you meet in the pine wood?"

Lydia gasped and splayed a hand across her chest.

"How do you know about that? No-one ever goes there. It's deep and dark and creepy."

"There's a gap in the brick wall and I saw him squeeze through," Judith explained. "I squeeze through, too, when I come to work.

"It's a mile quicker than taking the road right round to the rear gates and it doesn't scare me. We live on the edge of the oak wood opposite and I come through that, even in the dark of winter.

"But I took the long way round when I saw you both the other day. Can't you elope with him that way?" Her eyes widened with excitement.

Lydia gripped Judith's hand, her own eyes wide.

"What have you heard?"

"Nothing, miss. I read about elopements in the newspapers. Jinny and I think they're so romantic.

"Well, they're not. It's difficult to plan, especially when you're chaperoned all the while as I am." She stared forlornly over the garden.

"If you had a lady's maid, she could be your secret helper."

"Is that what you want to be, Judith, a lady's maid?"

"Yes." As if suddenly realising her current position, Judith stood up. "I should go, Miss Lydia. What if your governess catches me?"

"Maud is not my governess; she was Stepfather's old governess, which is why he put her in charge of me. I'm not allowed to speak to anyone while I'm here other than the fat marquis."

"I'll speak to you, miss. I'll be your friend."

"Thank you, Judith, but you mustn't risk your job. But if you would avoid the pine wood just until −"

"Lydia!" a woman's crowing voice yelled along the landing.

"Quick, Judith, under the bed."

Judith rolled under just as the bedroom door opened.

"There you are. I've been looking for you. I thought you were still with your stepfather." The black-garbed, grim-faced elderly spinster peered round the room suspiciously.

"I had a headache after that encounter," Lydia said, sitting on the bed with her gown spread to hide Judith. "I came to lie down. Would you fetch me a sleeping draught?"

She set a hand across her brow.

Leaving the door open, the governess crossed to her room opposite.

"Quick! And thank you for being my friend," Lydia hissed as Judith sneaked through the door to scuttle down the corridor to the servants' stairway as silently as her boots would allow.

\*   \*   \*   \*

Judith took the long way round the walls of the estate to get home that evening.

As she walked on through the oak wood, her mind was on Miss Lydia and what she had been about to tell her. Could it be she was eloping through the pine wood? But when?

As she entered the kitchen door her sister Jinny, who was eight years older, was stirring a vegetable stew. She'd been upgraded from cleaner to take her mum's place serving in the station café.

Judith, her mind still with Miss Lydia, began her chores by setting the table with three bowls and cutlery.

Jinny left her post and took one setting away.

"You mustn't keep pining over Mum, Judith."

Judith looked up.

"I wasn't. I was thinking of something else."

"Oh, dear. About us leaving?"

Judith gaped in surprise, and Jinny sat down at the table.

"I didn't want to tell you until I'd tried all angles. But it's no good. We haven't enough to pay the rent on this cottage now Mum's gone."

"Where are we going to live?"

"You know the old gentleman at the station who always had a word with Mum and me while waiting for his London train?

"I've known him a year now, and well, I was so upset when Mum died, he consoled me. Now, because I can read and write, he's offered me a job in his newspaper office in the city.

"He hasn't room or pay for both of us. But he'll find you a live-in position, doing what you're doing now. It's a start up that ladder Mum was always on at us about."

She beamed Judith a cheery smile.

That night in the bed they shared, Judith's mind wasn't on leaving the cottage. She didn't like working at the big house with that horrid master. Not many of the servants did.

Instead, she was thinking of Miss Lydia and her escape, which she was sure was being planned. She remembered reading of one particular elopement in a newspaper her mum had brought home some years ago.

The girls' learning had come from reading the happenings in the newspapers, cuddled in bed together. And this elopement had been so audacious it was the buzz of London for months after.

The newspapers were still piled in the corner of their bedroom. Judith was impatient to search through them for that story, but it was October and too dark to hunt till the morning.

She was dozing off when she heard the shots. She presumed it was poachers. Jinny groaned and slept on.

Suddenyl there was a loud, insistent knocking on the kitchen door. Within a minute Jinny was awake, throwing her robe on and heading down the stairs.

She gave a cry of alarm and shuffling sounds and subdued voices reached Judith. She put her robe on and slipped down to the kitchen.

Seated by the range was Miss Lydia's handsome beau. His temple was dripping blood. His hair was tangled, his face scratched, clothing and boots muddied.

"They were waiting for us when we −"

"I don't want to know," Jinny interrupted, pouring warm water into a dish from the kettle on the range. "Judith, go and check the front door then come back and watch for anyone coming."

Judith rushed off. She knew what had happened. Miss Lydia's elopement had failed.

Back at the kitchen window, she heard voices and saw lamplight twinkling through the woodland, heading closer.

"They're here!"

Jinny blew the lamp out. She gripped Judith to her. The young man sat at the table holding a wad of cloth against his temple, staring at the window, listening, too.

Judith jumped as lights flashed through the flimsy curtains, the voices fading as they moved on through the village.

Jinny lit the lamp, keeping it dim. Then she reached for a bandage.

"Thank you, but I'm less conspicuous without," he said. "I've been slack in my respect to you both. I'm Oliver −"

"I'll be grateful when you're fit enough to leave," Jinny said politely.

"I understand." He stood up. "Thank you both for your kindness."

He nodded to Jinny while Judith unlocked the rear door and looked out.

"All's clear." When he stepped out, she paused. "Can I give Miss Lydia a message?"

"You know her?" he said, astounded.

"I work at the big house." She glanced round to check Jinny was still clearing away the evidence.

"Just tell her not to give up hope, that I'll find a way," he said.

\*    \*    \*    \*

When Judith arrived at work, the kitchen was buzzing with gossip of how Miss Lydia was caught with her beau escaping through the wood.

Maud had found her bed unslept in, told the stepfather and he'd sent two of his guns after them.

Her beau was shot . . . wounded badly . . . dead. Now Miss Lydia was locked in her room, and Maud was with her, sleeping there, too, not letting her out of her sight.

That wasn't all. Miss Lydia was to be married to the Marquis of Walton this very Sunday!

Judith was alarmed. This was Thursday!

She carried on with her chores, which included laying a fire in Miss Lydia's room. But Maud stood over her, watching, while Lydia sat on the window seat across the room from her. She was weeping quietly.

Judith wished she could kick the old crow in the shins.

That evening, straight after her meal and her chores, Judith ran up to the bedroom. She began sorting through the newspapers.

Minutes later Jinny came in, to see Judith on the mat in a sea of them.

"What are you looking for?" she asked, setting a pile of freshly ironed linen on the bed.

"That story about Lady Denham eloping even though she was being chaperoned at the time."

"You're not thinking of showing it to Miss Lydia?" Jinny had heard the gossip of last night's escape.

"We're leaving anyway, so what does it matter?" Judith continued her frantic search.

"You mustn't get involved. It's dangerous for us, especially now we're leaving." Jinny cocked her head. "There's someone knocking on the door. Stay here."

Judith opened a drawer and found a clutch of cuttings under the clothing. She took out the relevant one and then followed her sister.

"What are doing here?" Jinny was asking Oliver, tugging him through the rear door in case he was spotted.

"I wondered if you or your sister had heard anything . . ."

"Miss Lydia's locked in her room," Judith told him. "Guarded night and day by the governess. The master is marrying Miss Lydia to the Marquis of Walton this Sunday."

"No!" He sank down at the table. "I've let her down. But the guns were sighted on me," he told them, looking between them. "Her stepfather wanted me dead. I had to leave her. My poor Lydia."

Jinny put a hand on his shoulder.

"I'm so sorry."

"I found the cutting." Judith handed it to Oliver. "It's about a posh lady who eloped, and she was well guarded, too."

He read it, then looked between them, eyes alight with hope.

"This could work. But time's short. How would we get a message to Lydia?"

"I know a way. Just write down the instructions for her." Judith grabbed pen and paper from the dresser.

"I wouldn't want you losing your job." Oliver's voice held concern.

"We're leaving here, so it doesn't matter," Judith replied, eager in her quest.

\* \* \* \*

On Friday morning Judith was laying a fire in the basket grate of Lydia's room.

Maud was hovering by the closed door, her eyes flashing from Lydia on the window seat to Judith across the room. She was taking no chances on them talking or touching.

Judith had set the coal scuttle to the left of the hearth, the far side from where the governess stood.

As she arranged the coals she pretended to drop some over the side of the scuttle. In reaching for them she set the missive under the edge of the rug.

As she got up and turned, her eyes met Lydia's, who gave a subtle nod.

On Saturday morning, as soon as Judith arrived in the kitchen Cook called her over.

"The master wants to see you in the library. What have you been up to?"

Judith didn't answer. It could only mean Maud had found the note. Judith didn't care if she lost her job. But poor Miss Lydia, there would be no time for another plan.

She rubbed her clammy hands down her black working dress as she stood outside the master's door. She knocked.

When he called for her to enter, she kept her head dipped as she walked to stand before the desk, hands clasped tightly.

The master looked her up and down.

"Your name, girl?"

"Judith, sir."

"You have a best dress at home?"

Judith looked up, surprised by the question.

"Yes, sir."

He leaned back in his chair, fingers laced, smiling superciliously.

"My stepdaughter is looking forward to her marriage tomorrow. She wishes to go to Hanley and Bowman's department store today for a full wedding trousseau.

"Maud is too frail to walk far, so I shall accompany her. But she has asked for a female companion to carry small items she may wish to bring home with her ahead of delivery of larger ones.

"And she wants you, as the youngest of the servants, to do that service. Remember, your job is at stake, so you will follow my instructions, not Miss Lydia's. Understand?"

"Yes, sir." Judith could hardly keep the smile from her face.

$$* \quad * \quad * \quad *$$

Because she was dressed so prettily in her pink dress with the satin sash, with her dark hair tied back with a satin ribbon, Judith was allowed to sit in the carriage opposite Miss Lydia and the master.

She was not to speak, but to keep her head lowered and sit quietly.

She was glad to obey, for if she met Miss Lydia's eye the game would be up.

And this was more than a game; it was Miss Lydia's future.

So far, everything was going to plan. Miss Lydia wore a slimline linen bodice and matching skirt, along with gloves and small hat, a suitably unhampered outfit for ease and speed.

As they stepped from the carriage at the entrance to the department store, the master spoke severely to Judith.

"You will not talk to Miss Lydia. You will walk quietly with your hands clasped in front of you, no gawping, touching or speaking to anyone!"

Judith, with her mother and Jinny, had wandered around this store, dreaming of what they would like to buy, but it was an even more thrilling experience today for Judith.

First, they headed up to ladies' fashions. The master sat in the viewing room while Lydia tried on the first wedding dress.

"I think this is perfect."

"Really?" her stepfather said, sitting up in his seat, surprised. Most women spent for ever choosing a dress.

But then, in this case, they only had today.

From evening gowns to furs, perfume, day dresses, jewellery, shoes, hats and purses, Lydia led them through every department.

And that was the plan. To tire him, especially his mind.

When, three hours later, the clock on the tower of the store chimed a quarter to one, she smiled.

"Lingerie now." She swirled off once again on her stepfather's arm, hurrying the tired man along.

Judith couldn't fault her nerve, but then, every minute was drawing her closer into the arms of Oliver and her freedom.

At the opening that led into the department Lydia turned and held her stepfather back.

"Gentlemen are not allowed in this department. See, there are seats in this alcove." She indicated one other jaded gentleman.

As her stepfather opened his month to speak, she gave him a comforting pat on his chest.

"It's the last call, then we can all go home. Judith can stay with you."

Judith was surprised. She was holding just two small packages.

"Thank you for your help, my dear, I shall always appreciate it." Lydia squeezed her hand before gliding off into the lingerie department.

Judith gave a small curtsey, and would have been disappointed at not seeing the escape through to its conclusion, but for the small folded paper Lydia had passed into her hand.

\*   \*   \*   \*

"Oh, you should have seen him, Jinny. He was apo . . . apo . . ."

"Apoplectic?" Jinny smiled as she leaned over her sister reading the newspaper on the table.

"Here, listen."

"Judith you've already read it to me twice."

Judith's forefinger slid along the lines of "The Sunday Times".

*There was outrage yesterday as heiress Miss Lydia Feltham eloped through Hanley and Bowman's department store.*

*She was buying her trousseau for her imminent marriage to the Marquis of Walton.*

*However, her true love, the Marquis of Trettington, was waiting at the rear entrance of the store with a carriage to whisk her away. They were married an hour later and have now travelled on to France.*

"'Miss Lydia's stepfather was left waiting for her so long he'd fallen asleep . . .'" Judith went on. "You hear that, Jinny? Oh, it was so funny. I watched him. After all, it wasn't my job to wake him."

She dug the note from her pocket.

*Write to me at this address. When we return, after the scandal has been forgotten, I'll have a position for you.*

"Hear that, Jinny? I'm on my way up Mum's ladder, too. Wouldn't she be proud of us?" ▧

# First Day At School

## by Eirin Thompson

**D**ID all mums feel like this, Leah wondered. It might be Joel's first day at school, but at least he'd have a teacher to tell him the rules.

It was a big first day for her, too, sending her only child out into the world, and if somebody somewhere knew all the guidelines for that, then they hadn't shared them with her.

Looking around her at the school gate, it seemed that all the other very small children were wearing those ties on elastic.

The man in the school uniform outfitters had offered Leah that option, but she had declined, thinking Joel might as well learn to tie a proper tie from the start. Now, she feared she'd made him the odd one out.

Mrs Nugent's information session, before the summer break, had included advice to bring new children to the classroom door and drop them there, being firm about not looking back if there were tears.

"It might sound brutal, but experience shows it's far more humane than dragging things out," Mrs Nugent had promised.

Leah had talked Joel through the expected scenario and had thought she'd prepared him well.

On arrival at the classroom, however, she found multiple parents blocking the doorway as they bade their children chatty and protracted goodbyes, and plenty more in the room, too.

"Just three more hugs and then Mummy has to go, Kaydee," one crouched figure was saying.

"Oh, look, Henry! Dinosaurs! Do you want to show me?" a dad suggested.

Mrs Nugent was settling two children down with some play-dough, and wasn't showing much concern about the intruding adults.

What was the right thing to do now? Follow Mrs Nugent's earlier instructions and firmly leave, or copy these other mums and dads?

Illustration by Martin Baines.

Leah didn't want anyone – especially Joel – to think she didn't care as much about her child as the other parents.

"Don't look so worried," a friendly voice said.

Leah turned to see a burly, slightly dishevelled man with a messy-looking little girl hanging on his arm.

"They're what I call the Gushing Brigade – they layer on the schmaltz with a trowel. It's like a competitive parental love-in."

Kaydee's mum must have overheard, because she turned and scowled.

"I might've known it was you, Felix. We don't all want our family life to resemble 'Lord Of The Flies', you know."

"She's crazy about me," Felix whispered to Leah knowingly. Leah thought he was joking, but she wasn't completely sure.

The wild-looking little girl swung herself energetically off her father's arm and bounded into the role-play area.

"Bye, honeybunch. Missing ya already!" Felix called in a fake voice.

"C'mon. Let's get out of here," he said to Leah. "I'll stand you a decaff, since I expect your nerves are shattered. First-timer, am I right?"

Leah nodded.

"Bye, buddy." He offered Joel a high five, which Joel accepted with a grin.

"Let's go, before Mrs Nugent begs me to marry her again," Felix said under his breath.

Leah wondered if he was just a little bit nuts.

"See?" Felix went on, as he and Leah strode off up the hallway. "Little chap was fine with you leaving – because you didn't behave like an idiot."

"I take it you've been through this before?" Leah replied.

"Several times," Felix agreed. "Magpie's our fourth – well, my fourth, I suppose, now that Caitlin's bowed out."

"Wow! There's a lot to unpack in that sentence," Leah observed. "First of all – Magpie? And second, you're a single dad of four?"

"Magpie's her name, all right. Caitlin and I were exhausted after she was born. We'd managed with three kids, but somehow having a fourth tipped us over some sort of line.

"We didn't have the energy to pick a name, so we asked the older three to do it. Jennifer said it wasn't her problem, and Frances wanted to call her Frances – she was three at the time — so we had to give the winning vote to Daisy, who chose Magpie.

"She pointed out that if you can name a child after a flower, you can name one after a bird. Logical, I suppose, plus we were too tired to argue. It kind of grows on you.

"The coffee place on the corner is decent enough — it does a good bacon sandwich."

"OK," Leah agreed.

She hadn't really been looking forward to spending the morning alone, fretting about Joel. Maybe having company would be a good thing,

At the café, Felix explained that Caitlin, his former partner, had been an artist, but not a very successful one, which left her having to spend most of her time working in arts administration instead of being creative.

She'd encountered an American gallery owner at an event, who had liked her work and offered her the chance to exhibit in the States.

The exhibition had been Caitlin's most successful by far and she and Felix had agreed to her taking a year out to see if she could build upon it over there.

Over the course of that year, Caitlin had developed not only a career Stateside, but also a home and a new relationship. After much soul-searching, she'd decided to stay.

"She comes back three or four times a year and spends time with the kids," Felix said. "But for the remainder they've just got me."

"I can't imagine trying to raise four children on my own," Leah said. "Joel feels like a lot, some days."

"You learn to cut corners," Felix admitted. "You might have noticed that Magpie didn't have French plaits, or a little sparkly clip.

"None of them have those fiddly, manicured sandwiches, either — they have big door-stops and, if they're picky, they can bring the crusts home for the dog."

"You have a dog as well!"

"Oh, yes. Secret Squirrel — he came ready-named from the pound. I don't know – a man called Felix, a girl called Magpie and a dog called Squirrel. Is it any wonder the other parents judge us?"

"I live in fear of being judged, as a parent," Leah confided.

"You mustn't think like that," Felix said, suddenly serious. "I bet you're a brilliant mum. Your little boy seemed confident, and he had a cracking smile – you acquire one of those through plenty of usage."

"I do think he's a lovely child, but then I'm biased," Leah replied.

"That's allowed." Felix looked at his watch. "Look, I'm going to have to shoot off and get some work done while they're all in school.

"It was nice meeting you, Leah. And please, be true to yourself – you don't want to end up like the others."

On her walk home, Leah didn't feel as bad as she'd expected, given the stresses of the day. She even took an hour to study job vacancies online.

She'd been thinking of looking for a new post once Joel started school, and if Felix could bring up four children on his own and hold down work, then surely she could manage something, too.

It wasn't the life she'd hoped for – she'd wanted a big family, and she certainly hadn't wanted Jamie to fall in love with her best friend, so that she lost them both.

But she was determined not to wallow, and instead to make the best of what opportunities she could seek out.

Soon it was time to return to school, collect Joel and hear how his first morning had gone. And Leah had to acknowledge that she was also looking forward to bumping into Felix again.

Joel beamed when he saw her at the playground gates.

Mrs Nugent beckoned her over and Joel ran into her arms,

"I painted a picture of a car and I wrote a 'J' for Joel!" he exclaimed,

"Well done!" Leah replied.

She looked questioningly to Mrs Nugent.

"Joel had a super morning, and he made a new friend."

"She's called Magpie. She's a girl. She has long hair. There she is!"

Leah looked round, expecting to see Felix, but instead Magpie was being taken away by the wrist by Kaydee's unsmiling mother.

"Typical Felix," she was muttering. "Always needing a favour. I should never have given him my mobile number.

"Can I help?" Leah asked. "I don't mind."

Mrs Nugent intervened.

"It's kind of you to offer but we can only release a child to someone authorised by a parent."

"Of course," Leah said, blushing.

This was another rule she hadn't been aware of, though she felt now it should have been obvious — she wouldn't expect the school to send Joel home with just anyone.

Whilst Joel had been thoroughly excited about his first day at school, he seemed genuinely surprised to hear that he was expected to repeat the activity the next day.

Leah found him more enthusiastic when she explained that Magpie would be there again, and would be every schoolday except if she was sick.

In the playground that second morning, she found Felix looking unexpectedly stressed.

"Childcare problems," he stated. "Daisy has an unexplained rash, so even though she seems perfectly well she can't go to school until it's been identified by a doctor. But I have an appointment this afternoon."

After the previous day's playground snub – however legitimate – Leah was hesitant about offering assistance.

But Felix took matters into his own hands.

"I don't suppose you could . . .?"

"I'd love to! I'll take her home with us, will I?"

Felix looked sheepish.

"I suppose there's no chance you could go to mine? It might be late when I get back and if someone could be there for the others . . ."

*　　*　　*　　*

Felix's house wasn't like something from a magazine. There were books everywhere, but not, Leah suspected, Marie Kondo's bestseller about the magic of tidying up.

Dirty dishes littered the kitchen benches. The tall pedal bin was overflowing. Piles of laundry – probably clean, though it was hard to tell when it was so rumpled – lined the bottom stairs.

Magpie pulled Joel into the middle of it and tipped out a biscuit tin full of little cars.

As Joel got stuck in, Leah resolved to do the same. She pushed up her sleeves, made everyone toast and hot chocolate, then started loading the dishwasher.

Some people might have thought it distinctly old-fashioned to take on a man's house, his children and all the domestic work that went along. But Leah had chosen not to bow to the judgement of others.

By becoming Felix's housekeeper, she gained a very decent salary for her trouble. Her employment also meant she was always there for Joel, and he got to play and share as part of a family.

It couldn't have worked out better, until Felix asked Leah to marry him, and then it did.

"Are you trying to save my wage for the one-off price of a wedding?"

"Yes," he replied, straight-faced.

In fact, Felix had given Leah his bank card that very first day and told her to spend whatever she needed. He was the most trusting and generous person she'd ever met.

"I'm also hoping that making an honest woman of you will stop the unrelenting attentions of Kaydee's mum and Mrs Nugent and all the many others."

"I'll have to consult Joel," Leah said, already sure of how her son would feel about joining his honorary family for real.

"Please do, and quickly," Felix replied. "I was going to ask him to be my best man!" ■

**B**RITISH director David Lean discovered Dickens's novel thanks to his wife insisting he accompany her to a stage production. He then wrote a screenplay and cast two members of that performance to play the same roles in the film. Martita Hunt played Miss Havisham and a young Alec Guinness, in his first major film role, played Herbert Pocket.

The film follows Pip, whose childhood encounter with criminal Magwitch changes the course of his life in ways that he will not appreciate for many years. He meets the eccentric Miss Havisham and her cruel young ward, Estella, with whom he falls in love.

A mysterious benefactor funds Pip's education in London to enable him to become a gentleman. Pip returns home as a young man (played by John Mills, then thirty-eight), hoping to win Estella's affections, but fate has other ideas.

The film was well received, winning Oscars for Best Direction and Best Cinematography and being nominated for three others (Best Picture, Best Director and Best Screenplay).

It became the third most popular film at the British box office in 1947 and was Canada's most popular movie of 1948.

*Donaldson Collection/Getty Images and iStock.*

# Jolly Jack Tar

## by Valerie Bowes

NOT witches. We've had witches."

"Scouts around a camp fire?"

"Been done."

"It gets harder to think of something original every year, doesn't it?" Sally sighed.

"I loved Jack Brownett's little guy getting his chips pinched by a seagull," Pippa recalled. "I'm not surprised it won first prize last time.

"But you're right, it does get harder. So, what are we going to do?"

The Scarecrow Festival was only three weeks away. Most of the village entered, and the scarecrows peering from every corner brought people from miles around.

They wandered the two streets to find them all, exclaiming and laughing at the quirky and the imaginative, and spent their money at the stalls selling snacks, local produce and crafts. It was a great weekend.

But what could Sally and her sister come up with to win the meal for two at the pub?

They'd nearly managed it last year, with the three witches dancing round a cauldron. But they'd come second to Jack's flying bird and chipless boy.

Sally had wondered who he'd take. She'd thought, at one time, that Jack's eye had brightened when he saw her and couldn't help wondering if it might be her that he asked.

As far as she knew, he wasn't in a relationship; he just had a succession of friends. Much the same as her.

She wouldn't have said no if he'd asked her out at any time, let alone to the winning meal. But he'd taken a girl from work.

The chef at the Carpenter's Arms insisted on the freshest produce, sourced from local growers and farmers, and was making quite a name for himself, the pub and the village.

Pippa had been and was enthusiastic, although Sally hadn't yet tried it. They could go any old time they wanted, but it was the thrill of

*Illustration by Philip Crabb.*

winning that was the real prize.

And, Sally wondered, would that make Jack see her as more than just the girl from his village whom he'd known all his life?

"What's Jack doing this year, do you know?" she asked casually.

Pippa shrugged.

"Haven't heard. I know the lads from Number Thirty-five are doing a pirate ship by the flagpole in the square."

"So, what are we going to do?"

In the end, they decided to do a village maiden. Sally had a pretty dress that was past its best but, with a bit of adjustment, would make a Victorian young lady happy.

It was ankle length, and a delicate shade of blue and lilac check.

"We'll give her a shawl, put a wreath of flowers round her head and hang a basket of fruit over her arm," Pippa enthused. "She can stand by the gate, as if she's waiting for a sweetheart."

The pillows that made up the body were stuffed with straw and Sally sewed long sausage shapes with gloves on the ends for the arms. Pippa painted a face on a piece of sheeting and put a long golden wig on the maiden's head before she was tied to a stake hammered into the ground by the gate,

"There you go. Pretty as a picture," Sally said.

Pippa tilted her head to one side and half closed her eyes.

"She looks almost as if she's real. Pity we won't have time to make a sweetheart for her."

"Let's go and see what everyone else is doing," Sally suggested. "Most of them will be up by now. Judging's tomorrow."

"OK," Pippa said, glancing at her watch, "but I can't be long. I've got a shift at Wattendon at two o'clock."

That year's crop of scarecrows was brilliant.

Sally and Pippa laughed at the one outside the pub looking distinctly worse for wear, and had to hide a smile as they said hello to Mavis Haddon when they passed her.

Bill Haddon had done a scarecrow that was reclining in a deckchair reading the paper, with his hand resting on a small table on which was a glass of beer. All the village knew that Mavis would never let Bill do that!

They were admiring the pirate ship when Pippa glanced at her watch and let out a small shriek.

"Got to go! Chef'll go doolally if I'm late."

Pippa was training to be a chef and Sally knew she would really like to work in the kitchen of the Carpenter's. Maybe, if they won the prize, it might give her the courage to ask the chef there for a job.

But there was one scarecrow they hadn't got around to, and it was the one that Sally most wanted to see.

Although Jack had a tiny flat in the town where he worked, he always stayed with his mum when he came back to the village.

Mrs Brownett's cottage was the last in the street. Sally headed that way, wondering if he had got his entry finished yet.

As she approached, she could see a head poking over the wall, a sailor's cap jauntily tipped over one eye. Jack was just putting the final touches to the support and looked up as he heard her footsteps.

"Like him?" he asked, tweaking the broad, white-lined handkerchief into a better position.

"He looks very handsome. Jolly Jack Tar, with a girl in every port! Any relation?" Sally smiled, thinking she'd seen him with so many girls she'd lost count.

"All the nice girls love a sailor!" Jack pointed out. "Although I'll have to trim that straw a bit. I can just hear the CPO telling him to 'get 'is 'air cut!'"

"So long as he's not a Drunken Sailor! Have you seen the scarecrow that's outside the pub? Definitely three sheets to the wind!"

"No, I haven't seen any of them yet. I only got home last night. Fancy giving me the Grand Tour?"

Sally could think of nothing she'd like better, but just then Mrs Brownett came bustling out.

"Hello, Sally, dear. Ah, there you are, Jack! Would you have time to run me into Wattendon? I don't know where the time's gone this morning, but it's not where I left it and I'll be awfully late otherwise."

"Of course, Ma." Jack sent an apologetic glance at Sally,

"No worries. I'll see you at the judging," she said.

She looked back at the sailor as she left. He was trying to live up to the Jolly Jack bit, with the rakish tilt to his cap, but she wasn't so sure.

She couldn't help feeling there was a sadness about his eyes that was at odds with the painted cheery grin.

\*　\*　\*　\*

Here it was, the Day of Judgement, but there was no village maiden standing by the gate!

Sally shook her head in disbelief as she went down the path, with a wreath of flowers ready to put on the scarecrow's head and a basket of fruit to hang on her arm.

Why hadn't she checked to see all was well long before this? Maybe the maiden had fallen over, but she couldn't see the pale blue and lilac dress lying in the grass.

Perhaps someone had stood her up again somewhere else. Or Pippa had moved her.

Sally couldn't think why her sister would have done so unless the support had broken and the maiden had indeed fallen over.

"Pip!" she called, running back to shout up the stairs. "Pip, have you moved the maiden?"

There was no answer. Come to think of it, she hadn't seen or heard anything of her sister this morning, but that was nothing unusual.

Pippa usually had a lie-in after she'd been slaving over a hot stove late into the evening.

The maiden wasn't lying under the hedge or propped against the wall. Sally juggled the wreath and basket as she glanced up and down the street, expecting to hear someone giggling at their prank.

What she did see was the judging party appraising the scarecrow from two doors down. They'd be here in a minute, and there was nothing for them to see.

She ran down the road, searching the gardens for any glimpse of blue and lilac. The only scarecrows she could see were the legitimate residents, but coming back up the other street, she heard her name being called.

Jack was standing by his gate, looking bemused.

"Brilliant idea, Sally, but when did you do it? It wasn't like this when I went to bed last night."

Jolly Jack Tar was standing where Sally had seen him yesterday.

But he was leaning forward holding the hands of the village maiden, who was propped against the other side of the wall. Their faces were close, as though they were about to kiss.

"I didn't," she said, showing him the flowers and the basket. "She wasn't in the garden when I went to put her wreath on. I've been looking for her everywhere."

"Well, someone must have done it," he said.

"I'll bet it was Pippa," Sally said, remembering the knowing look her sister always had when she saw Jack and Sally together.

Her idea of a subtle hint?

Jack reached out a hand to open the gate for her.

"Here come the judges. Come in, quick! Let's put her flowers on but you'd better leave that basket by her feet. She seems to have got her hands rather full at the moment!"

The judges smiled as they consulted their clipboards.

"Sweethearts!" Jack said, laughing. "Not you. Them."

"But we've got him down as Jolly Jack Tar," the man said, puzzled.

"With a girl in every port," Sally said quickly.

"Beautifully done," the lady commented as they ticked boxes and turned away.

"Right, just a couple more to see, then the results will be announced this afternoon. We hope to see you both then."

Sally let out the breath she'd been holding. Beside her, Jack seemed to be doing the same.

"Whoever moved her did us a favour," he said. "Now I want to see the rest. You do realise you haven't given me the Grand Tour yet?"

Without any conscious thought, she reached out and caught his hand.

"Come on, then. You'll love Bill Haddon's!"

He squeezed her fingers.

"I don't know about you, but I reckon we've a good chance of winning. Just in case we don't, though, would you have dinner with me at the Carpenter's anyway?" He stopped abruptly and looked at her. "That is – unless you're still going out with Stephen Lang?"

Sally stared at him.

"I never was."

"Really? I've seen you together every time I've been home."

"We were helping with the archaeology up on Holme Hill, that's all. And I'd love to have dinner with you."

He swung her hand with a smile as broad as Jolly Jack's.

"That's settled, then. Let's go and suss out the opposition."

I must remember to thank Pip, Sally thought.

But, just then, a car pulled up and Pippa tumbled out.

"Am I in time? Hey, why's our maiden making up to a sailor?"

Sally frowned.

"Didn't you move her?"

"I didn't get home last night. It was so late when we finished, they gave me a room at the pub. The manager's just brought me back."

The maiden couldn't have come to find her lover, could she? Reason said not, but Sally could swear Jolly Jack's eyes had lost their sadness.

The sailor and the maiden had found their true loves at last, and maybe they weren't the only ones. ◼

*Illustration by Jim Dewar.*

# The Tunnel Of Love

## by Linda Lewis

EVERLEY stared out of the window of the train, barely acknowledging the beautiful Devon countryside as it rushed past. The weekend had been over before she'd had time to really relax. At the age of fifty-nine she was head over heels in love.

Her instinct was to shout it to the world but she couldn't risk upsetting her family, and all the secrecy was starting to get her down.

She glanced at her watch. Only another 46 minutes and she'd be back in the real world.

She closed her eyes and let herself relive the last two days, days filled with love rather than piles of dirty washing and endless housework and cooking.

A man's voice interrupted her musings.

"Is this seat taken?"

She looked up to see a figure standing in the gangway, his head a silhouette against the light.

"No. It's free. Help yourself," she said.

While he put his coat on the overhead shelf, Beverley tucked her bag under her feet, then closed her eyes once more.

"I'm going to Exeter," he said.

Beverley nodded and smiled. The last thing she wanted was a conversation with a stranger but the man didn't take the hint.

"How about you?" he asked. "Where are you headed?"

"Exeter," she replied without opening her eyes.

However hard she tried, she couldn't get back into her daydream. That other life, the one she only lived when she could get away for a couple of days, was already drifting out of reach.

With a sigh, she gave up and pulled out a book.

"Snap," the man said.

"Sorry?" When she turned towards him, she saw he was holding exactly the same novel – Lee Child's latest thriller.

For the first time, she looked at him properly.

She guessed he was in his seventies but there was something about him that made him appear a lot younger. He had the most wonderful Johnny Depp cheekbones and eyes so blue and full of sparkle, they made her think of sapphires.

"Is it any good?" he asked. "My daughter recommended him."

"I'm only halfway through," she replied.

Pointedly, she opened the book and began to read but it proved impossible. It was clear to her that the man was hiding something behind his smile, that he was desperate for somebody to talk to.

She put her book back in her bag.

"My name's Beverley."

"Ken." He offered his hand. "Pleased to meet you."

For the next 10 minutes, hardly stopping to draw breath, he gave her his potted life history. He'd married at the age of nineteen, and they'd gone into business together, building a two-person catering business into a thriving enterprise.

As he spoke about his wife, Beverley could hear the love in every syllable of every word he spoke.

"Laura died two years ago," he said softly.

"I'm so sorry," Beverley said.

"It was like losing part of myself. We were together for fifty-three years. In all that time, I never even looked at another woman."

He chuckled.

"OK, that's a lie. I looked. All men do, but nothing more. Laura was all I ever wanted in life."

Beverley wasn't used to people speaking so openly about their feelings. In her family, people tended to bottle things up.

"The weather's been nice," she said.

Ken laughed.

"Changing the subject. I see. So what takes you to Exeter?"

"I live there."

It turned out that he knew the area well, having attended school there.

"There's a lovely park not that far from you. Princes, I think it's called."

"You must mean Pinces Park," she said.

"That's right! There used to be a tunnel made of wisteria. It really was the most marvellous sight. And the smell – so thick and heavy and sweet, you could almost feel it in the air."

Beverley nodded, though she hadn't been to the park for decades.

"How about you?" she asked. "What brings you to Exeter?"

He leaned closer and lowered his voice.

"I'm meeting a woman I met on a dating site. We've been exchanging messages for several weeks. Today, we're finally going to meet."

"Wow!" Beverley said. "Aren't you nervous?"

"I'm absolutely terrified," Ken admitted with a chuckle. "I kept putting it off – I was sure my children wouldn't approve. When I finally mentioned it to my daughter last week, she gave me a right talking to."

His voice went up as he imitated his daughter's voice.

"You're only seventy-four, you've got years ahead of you. Mum wouldn't want you to be on your own so go and meet this woman. No expectations. See what happens." He smiled.

"I couldn't argue with anything she said." Again he lowered his voice. "I wouldn't dare, if I'm honest; she's so like her mother."

He took out his phone and showed Beverley photos of his family.

"They look so similar," she said. "Isn't that hard for you?"

He shook his head.

"It was at first. Now I see Laura in my daughter's eyes and it's as if she's still here."

Overhead, the Tannoy crackled into life.

"This is me," Ken said.

Beverley was about to say me, too, but changed her mind.

"Good luck," she said.

"Thank you. You, too." He pulled his coat from the shelf and sat back down. "Let an old man give you some advice – it's the things we don't do in life that we come to regret, not the things we do." He chuckled.

"That's why I'm meeting a strange woman in just under an hour."

Beverley watched Ken as he stepped down on to the platform. He took a moment to straighten his jacket, then headed for the exit with confident strides.

"Good luck," she said again, even though she knew he could no longer hear her.

She stayed on the train until it reached Exeter St Thomas. There, she let her feet take her to Pinces Park.

The wisteria had finished blooming months ago but the tunnel was still there, just as she remembered it, with a lush green network of thickly twisting stems and trunks supporting the foliage.

The memory was so clear, she could smell the heavy perfume, hear the murmur of the bees and feel the sweet touch of Phil's lips on hers.

She thought about their marriage and where it had gone wrong. For the first couple of years after the divorce, she'd put all the blame on him, but now she knew that was unfair.

They'd been very happy until the children came along. After that, she'd become so wrapped up in them she barely noticed when Phil began spending more time at work.

Eventually, all the closeness they'd shared simply vanished. When he told her about his brief affair with a colleague, she was more relieved than surprised.

She left the park, phoned for a taxi and headed for home.

"It's me," she called out as she stepped through the door.

She took her case up the stairs. Her nineteen-year-old son's door was open so she risked a peek inside. As usual, he was stretched out on the bed, absorbed in a game on his laptop.

Her daughter's room was empty. Lately she'd been spending more time at her boyfriend's than she did at home.

Beverley went back downstairs to make herself some tea.

The laundry basket in the corner was overflowing. While the kettle boiled, she sorted through the pile and put a batch on to wash.

Her phone buzzed.

*Home yet?* the text read.

She called him straight back.

"I stopped off at Pinces Park. Where we . . ."

"Where we shared our first kiss." His voice caught. "I love you, Beverley. Always have, always will."

"I know. And I love you, too," she said.

A year ago, Phil had sent her a message on Twitter.

*I miss you* was all it said, but from the way her heart thumped as she read those three little words, she knew she'd never stopped loving him.

They'd met for a coffee. Two hours went by and neither wanted to leave. They'd been seeing each other as often as they could ever since.

She wanted to tell her children but was afraid they wouldn't approve. The break-up had hit them so hard they'd chosen not to have any contact with their father.

Now Phil had asked her to move in with him.

She thought about the man on the train, stepping into the unknown. It's the things we don't do that we regret, he'd said.

"Come round tomorrow evening," she said. "We need to tell the children that I'm seeing you."

"Are you sure?" he asked. "What if they're not happy about it?"

Maybe the children would surprise her, but even if they didn't, this was her chance of happiness and she wanted to grab it with both hands.

"We won't know until we tell them. I'm tired of sneaking about. I want us to be together."

As she put down the phone, Beverley made a vow. Come spring, they'd go back to Pinces Park and kiss under the wisteria the way they did many years before, without caring who saw them, or what anyone thought. ■

# Christ Church, Oxford

Christ Church is sandwiched between a vibrant city centre and lush, peaceful green meadow, the setting as diverse as the academic community. Oxford is the oldest university in Britain and remains one of the best. Stephen Hawking and Oscar Wilde number among the elite who have attended.

The City of Dreaming Spires has, unsurprisingly, been the perfect atmospheric backdrop for TV shows such as "Inspector Morse" and the Harry Potter movies, and wide streets offer an array of restaurants to suit every palate, while the covered market showcases the very best in local foods, drink and crafts.

Visit the botanic gardens or join a walking tour to learn more about this fascinating city which perfectly blends the old and new. From respecting long-held traditions to embracing new ways of thinking, Oxford is varied and fun. With museums and exhibitions, events and festivals, it's little wonder it holds so much appeal.

# Moonstruck

## by Annie Harris

I NTER-COUNTY Trains apologise for the further delay to the eighteen-fifty service to Oxenbury.
"The train is now scheduled to depart at nineteen-twenty, but because of the continuing transmission problems, passengers should use the rear carriage only."

The small group spread out along the platform, well apart from each other, muttering under their collective breaths. Then, as a chill gust of autumn wind sent leaves chasing across the rails, they huddled even further into their coats.

"Look, Mummy!" A small girl was pointing to a belt of trees on the far side of the station whose branches were being tossed to and fro. "The trees are dancing."

Her mother looked harassed and bent further over her phone.

"Look, Mummy," the child repeated more loudly. "They are!"

And a dark-haired young man, clutching his phone to his ear, clicked his tongue in irritation and moved further down the platform.

"At last!" someone muttered, as two yellow eyes appeared round the bend of the track and the small local train snaked into sight.

The first two carriages were in darkness so all the waiting passengers clambered into the last compartment, still ignoring each other as they settled back with sighs of relief.

The train juddered then finally lurched away from the station. Most of the adults at once returned to their phones, apart from one man who unfolded his newspaper and started work on the crossword, and the child, who began singing quietly to the teddy she was holding.

The middle-aged woman sitting across the aisle caught her eye and smiled at her.

"That's a nice teddy. I like his red coat. What's his name?"

"She's a lady bear," the child said promptly. "She's called Olivia."

"That's a really good name for a teddy. What's your name?"

"I'm called Lucy." She gave an enormous yawn. "I'm tired, Mummy."

"I know, love. We'll soon be home now," her mother replied, but her eyes were still fixed on her small screen. Sensing the older woman's silent reproach, she whispered, "My mum was rushed into hospital today with a serious heart attack. She's being operated on now."

"Oh, I'm so sorry."

"I wanted to stay." Her voice trembled. "But Dad said I must get home

*Illustration by Jim Dewar.*

with this one." She nodded down at her daughter, who was engrossed in buttoning her bear's jacket. "He's going to let me know."

She bit her lip and the woman leaned across and put her hand on her arm.

"I'm sure she'll be all right," she said. "They can do marvellous things these days."

The train jolted again, then came to a halt, and the guard's voice crackled over the speaker.

"I'm sorry, ladies and gentlemen, but the problem has recurred. We'll be on the move again as soon as possible."

There was a universal groan and the passengers rolled their eyes at each other, then retreated into their own private worlds.

A heavy silence fell.

"Mummy, Mummy! Look at the moon – it's ginormous. Look!"

At the insistent voice, all the passengers lifted their eyes, fingers poised in mid-air, and peered out. There were several gasps of amazement.

"It's incredible, isn't it?" one young woman said to no-one in particular.

The full moon, shining down into the carriage, was truly enormous. It was a pale rosy gold and its rays bathed the countryside as far as they could see in a luminous glow.

"It's the harvest moon," a young man said. "My grandad worked on a farm and he told me they used to work long into the night at this time of year, getting in the harvest."

"I know a poem about the moon – I learned it at school." The crossword-solving man laid his paper aside and smiled at Lucy. "Would you like to hear it?"

"Oh, yes, please. I like poems."

"Now, let me think. How did it go? Oh, yes. 'Slowly, silently, now the moon Walks the night in her silver shoon'."

"What's shoon?"

"I think that's a funny word for shoes."

"Shoon," the child repeated, then giggled. "I like that. I've got blue shoon – look." She held out a small foot for his inspection. "What comes next?"

"'This way and that –' er – oh, dear . . ."

"'This way and that, she peers, and sees Silver fruit upon silver trees'," the middle-aged woman sitting across from them put in quietly.

"That's it!" The man beamed at her. "Well done."

She shrugged.

"I learned it at school, like a lot of people in those days." She smiled at some far-off memory. "Miss Bates used to make sure we learned a poem a week."

"Miss Bates?" The man gazed at her, open-mouthed. "What school did you go to?"

"Hillfield Infant and Junior."

"So did I. Small world." They smiled at each other, weighing up their respective ages. "You'll remember Miss Hargreaves, then. But no," he added gallantly, "you're far too young."

"Oh, but I do." She laughed. "I certainly remember her. She was a tartar, wasn't she? Terrified the life out of us."

"You can say that again." He grinned. "One day – I must have been about ten – I chased a girl into the boys' toilet as a dare and old Hargreaves caught me and gave me a right telling-off." He wrinkled his brow. "Actually, I really fancied that girl. What was her name . . ."

"Janet Davies."

"That's right!" He stared across at her.

She laughed.

"It was me!"

"Good grief. Yes, of course, I can see it now. You've worn well. Much better than me," he added ruefully, then glanced at her hand. "Married, I see."

"Well, I was. Jim died three years ago."

"I'm sorry."

"Life has to go on, doesn't it? Although – I've just been staying with my daughter and her family. They have two children: Giles is eight and Leah's six."

"That's nice for you."

"Well, yes. But actually it's been a farewell visit as they're emigrating to Canada – Toronto. They think there'll be a lot more opportunities there, especially for the children."

He nodded.

"They could be right there – but it's tough for you."

"Yes. Jenny has tried to persuade me to up sticks and move with them, but well, we'll have to see. Anyway, how about you? Are you married?"

"No." He grimaced. "A messy divorce, six years ago. The old story – I was working too hard, too long hours, away from home a lot. For both of us, of course, but Pat got tired of it."

"I'm sorry, Bob."

"You remember my name?" He sounded delighted.

"Robert Hunt." She grinned. "Miss Hargreaves shouted it out often enough."

Their laughter was cut short as a young woman, sitting across the aisle, gave a stifled exclamation and the other passengers, who had been busy trying to pretend they hadn't been listening to the conversation, turned now to look at her.

She was struggling with tears.

"Are you all right?" the young man facing her asked.

"Oh – oh, yes." She gave him a watery smile. "It's just – I went for an interview earlier and they said they'd let me know. I really wanted the job but I've just heard I haven't got it."

There was a murmur of sympathy from round the carriage and the older woman reached forward to pat her arm.

"What job was it?" she asked.

"I've just finished my training as a legal secretary. There were three others for interview who were much more experienced than me so I suppose I was silly even applying."

"You've got all the qualifications though, I suppose." The young man, who had been giving her covert looks throughout the journey, taking in the dusting of freckles across her nose, was now eyeing her more openly.

"Oh, yes – I got good grades in all the exams."

"Well," he said slowly, "I hope I'm not jumping the gun, but I completed my law school training earlier this year and I'm joining my uncle's practice – Earl's, in the high street.'

"Yes, I know it."

"I'm another Earl – Connor."

"Megan Moore.'

"Pleased to meet you, Megan." He leaned across and they shook hands. "I'm going to be needing a legal secretary.

"You'd have to be interviewed, of course, and be up against those other applicants again with all their experience . . ." his brown eyes twinkled ". . . but there's nothing to stop you applying.

"If want to e-mail me I'll let you know when the job goes up."

Several of the other passengers exchanged covert smiles as they exchanged addresses. The train started moving and a muffled cheer went up.

But then the young mother suddenly stood up and went to the far end of the carriage where she could be heard speaking into her phone.

She returned after a few minutes and sank back into her seat.

"Everything all right, dear?" Janet asked tentatively.

"Yes, thank you – well, I hope so." She looked round at the concerned faces. "Mum's come through the op and she's conscious."

There was a general murmur of pleasure.

"I'm going back up tomorrow." She sighed. "Another long day for Lucy, I'm afraid, but we'll be all right, won't we, Lu?" She hugged the little girl fiercely.

"Where do you live?" Janet asked.

"On the new estate. We've got a maisonette on South Road. We've only just moved in."

"That's just a few minutes' walk from me – I'm in Lilac Crescent." Janet hesitated. "You don't know me, of course, but I'm the playgroup assistant at St Michael's and I'm fully PVG checked.

"Do you think Lucy would like to spend the day with me? In fact, I'll be at playgroup tomorrow – Lucy can come, too."

The woman's tired face lit up.

"That's really kind but we couldn't possibly impose on you."

"No, no. I'd love to have her. I've got all the toys my grandchildren play with – well, used to play with. And I'll be baking gingerbread men in the morning so Lucy could help me make them."

The girl stared at her, solemn-eyed.

"Can I scrape out the bowl?"

"Of course you can, my sweet." She turned to the mother again. "I'm making them for the playgroup."

"You'd like that, wouldn't you, Lu?"

"I think so," she said slowly. "Can Olivia come?"

"Of course she can." Janet laughed. "And she can help with the gingerbread men, too."

"Ladies and gentlemen, we shall shortly be arriving at Hampton. Inter-County Trains apologise once again for the delay. Thank you for your patience and have a good evening."

"What's left of it," Bob said to general laughter.

Then, as the train drew into the station, he picked up Janet's case and helped her down on to the platform.

Connor and Megan got off together and she stopped at the cycle rack.

"Where are you heading?" he asked.

"I've got a flat in Market Street, above the bookshop."

"That's on my way. Pop your bike in my car boot."

"Are you driving?" Bob asked Janet.

"No, but it's only a few minutes' walk."

"Nonsense. I'll take you." He turned to the young woman. "And your little one's out on her feet. So come on, hop in, everybody."

The sound of the cars died away and the platform fell silent.

The only movement was Mr Jenks, the stationmaster's tabby cat, who sat gazing up at the moon as it shone benignly down. ■

**H**ORROR has always been a Hollywood staple and audiences flocked to this 1946 shocker.

The spooky tale is based on a 1928 story by William Fryer Harvey, a Yorkshireman and practising Quaker who had served in the Friends Ambulance Unit during World War I – an interesting origin for such a dark story!

In the film, the studios' favourite sinister villain, Peter Lorre, plays Hillary Cummins, the neurotic friend of virtuoso pianist Francis Ingram, whose right side is now immobile after a stroke.

Ingram has withdrawn from public life, retiring to his isolated Italian manor with his nurse and a few close friends. When he dies in suspicious circumstances two wills are uncovered. Ingram's nephew and Cummins benefit from one; his nurse from the other.

As other members of the household are attacked or murdered, a ghostly disembodied hand is seen around the manor and the sound of Ingram playing the piano is heard, though there is no-one at the instrument . . .

The film was praised for its excellent special effects and for being genuinely scary.

# Modern Magic

## by Laura Tapper

THIS is always harder than you think." Tanya used her right hand to steady her left as she drew triangles and zigzags with a thin black marker.

She picked up the knife from the kitchen table and cut through the tough orange rind on the top of the huge vegetable.

"Be careful, darling." Her mother, at the far end of the table, peered out from between her fingers. "Nobody wants a trip to Casualty with a body part packed in ice, when there's so much still to be done before the children get home from school."

Tanya rolled her eyes.

"Thanks for your concern."

"You might be thirty-whatever-you-are . . ."

"Thirty-six, in January."

Tanya supplied the information while scooping moist flesh and flat seeds out into a bowl, using a huge, heavy spoon which had belonged to her great-grandmother.

It was her family's only heirloom and had been used for everything over the years from mixing bread dough to serving salad.

"You're still my little girl. As your three get older, you'll realise that you never stop worrying about them."

"I'm hoping it all gets a bit easier, though. At the moment, Kieran is an accident looking for a place to happen, and Joshua is like a bucket full of frogs.

"You'd think Harriet would be better, being the eldest, but no matter what she's doing, she's always got her mind on something else."

"Like mother, like daughter. Give her time — she's only seven."

"Seven going on seventeen."

They were quiet while Tanya did the tricky bit of carving out the features. At length, she turned the pumpkin round and held it up.

"There. How's that?"

*Illustration by iStock.*

"Perfect! I think it's even better than last year!"

Tanya beamed. She was so pleased that they'd worked out a way for her mother to be here to help with the preparations, and she knew it would make such a difference to the children.

Simon, their dad, was working away and wouldn't be back for another two weeks, so she wanted to make Hallowe'en fun.

"Right, now for the treasure hunt." Tanya slid a set of small cards towards her.

Each one had a seasonal symbol in the corner of it: a bat, a witch on a broomstick, a spider or a Jack-o-lantern.

"I've got little packets of spooky sweets, some pencils, stickers and other bits and pieces. I can hide them around the house. We just need the clues."

Her mother tapped the side of her head.

"They're all in here."

"I was hoping you'd say that. You shout them out and I'll write them down."

When Tanya was a child, her mother had always set up the best games for her to play.

She'd been an only child and so had her mother, so there were no cousins to come over at Christmas and birthdays, no siblings to play with on rainy days.

Thanks to her mother's ingenuity and youthful sense of fun, Tanya had never felt left out or lonely.

On the contrary, she looked back on her childhood as one full of laughter, excitement and just the right amount of silliness.

"Let's start simple, so that poor Joshua has a chance. It's not easy being the littlest and I've seen how hard he tries to keep up with the others.

"How about, 'To find your first clue, it must be said, go and look where you lay your head'."

"Under his pillow!" Tanya immediately started writing. "I'm sure he'll guess it."

"If not, you can whisper in his ear to help him along his way." There was a twinkle in her mother's eye, which showed the soft spot she had for her youngest grandchild.

Once the clues and treats had been spread throughout the house, they turned their attention to the decorations.

A witch's den was set up the back room, hung with cobwebs and draped with black fabric.

There was a large silhouette cut from black card of a witch bending over a cauldron and Tanya set a light up on the floor which was angled to throw an eerie shadow of the sinister-looking lady on to the wall behind.

"It's a good job my bunch don't scare easily!" Tanya laughed as she stretched to pin a string of paper bats to the ceiling, wobbling on the dining chair she was using instead of steps.

"You mind what you're doing! I can't catch you if you fall and those children need you, what with Simon working on the rigs."

"I know, Mum." Tanya didn't need reminding that all her support was an ocean away.

Decorations finished, it was time to lay out the Hallowe'en feast.

The lantern took pride of place in the centre of the table, and it was surrounded by a range of spooky fare: witches' fingers, made from cocktail sausages with pieces of Red Leicester for nails; ghost-shaped toasts with tomato dip; monster-face open sandwiches; cheese bones; and graveyard cupcakes.

There was a choice of witches' brew or frankenshake to drink and it was all spread on a paper tablecloth which had designs the children could colour in.

On the back of each chair, Tanya hung a mask which would cover the top part of their faces but leave their mouths free for eating. She stepped back and surveyed the scene with satisfaction.

"There, that should keep them happily occupied for five minutes!"

There was the pounding of feet on the path outside.

"We're ready just in time. Thanks for your help, Mum. Speak to you later."

Tanya blew her mother a kiss and went to open the front door.

"Hi, Mum!" was the general cry, as three dishevelled children trooped in, dumping their school bags and kicking off their shoes as they went.

"Thanks for picking them up, Ellie. I'll collect your two next Wednesday, when you've got the dentist. Was everything all right?"

"No worries. Any time, you know that. They seem very excited about Hallowe'en, but they say they're not going trick or treating."

"Would you like us to pop round when we've done, so Jake and Sam can share their haul with them?"

"No, that's fine – they've got a couple of calls they won't want to miss. But thanks ever so much for the offer."

The other mum nodded.

"OK, if you're sure. See you on the school run tomorrow, then – if we all survive the sugar fest!"

For an hour and a half, the house resounded with children having fun together, thundering up and down the stairs following clues, jumping out from behind furniture in their masks, eating spooky food and playing traditional Hallowe'en games.

Tanya saved their favourite until last and they were thrilled when the washing-up bowl was filled with water and placed on a chair, with the bathmat underneath in case of accidents.

Being the oldest, Harriet went first and caught a small apple on her second try.

"You must have been practising in the sink!"

Kieran was struggling to catch anything and flicked water on his sister before dipping down for another attempt.

At last he caught a Golden Delicious and then they all gathered around to watch Joshua have his first attempt at apple bobbing.

He tried and tried but, whenever he got close, the fruit dodged away from his little mouth.

Tanya took pity on him and, unseen by the rest of the group, she put her hand in the water and encouraged the apple to stay in place long enough for him to sink his teeth in.

For a moment, the reflection of his eyes caught hers in the water and she winked at him. She knew it was exactly what his grandma would have done if she could have been there.

At last, they all curled up together on the sofa with a tablet. First of all, a precious Hallowe'en video call from their dad, surrounded by the rest of the crew on the rig in a range of masks and all howling like werewolves.

Josh ducked behind the cushion, but Tanya coaxed him out. Then, they had a chat with Grandma, who was five hours behind them in Toronto where she was spending a year working at the university.

"Have you had a spooky time, then?" she asked them.

"It was epic! Some of the treasure hunt clues were really hard, but I guessed them all in the end." Harriet sounded proud of herself.

"Well, you are the oldest and a very clever girl. I think you take after your mother."

"Or maybe her grandmother," Tanya said.

"And I caught an apple in the bowl, all by myself!" Joshua puffed his

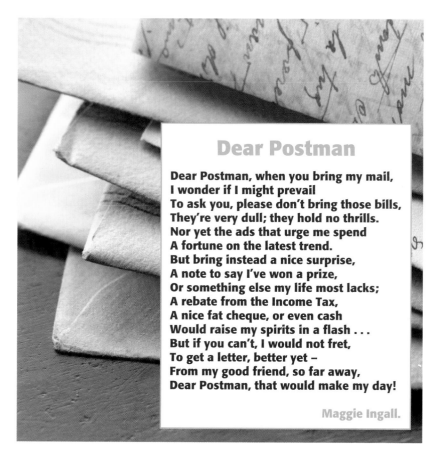

### Dear Postman

Dear Postman, when you bring my mail,
I wonder if I might prevail
To ask you, please don't bring those bills,
They're very dull; they hold no thrills.
Nor yet the ads that urge me spend
A fortune on the latest trend.
But bring instead a nice surprise,
A note to say I've won a prize,
Or something else my life most lacks;
A rebate from the Income Tax,
A nice fat cheque, or even cash
Would raise my spirits in a flash . . .
But if you can't, I would not fret,
To get a letter, better yet –
From my good friend, so far away,
Dear Postman, that would make my day!

Maggie Ingall.

little chest out.

"That's my boy! And how about you, Kieran?" "It was the best Hallowe'en ever!" He hesitated and his cheeks flushed. "I mean, it can't be exactly the best, because you and Dad weren't here, but it feels like you were, somehow . . ." His face was full of distress.

Tanya put her arm around him.

"Don't worry, we know what you mean. It's the wonder of technology – we can be together, even when we're apart."

"Can I kiss Grandma goodnight, then?" Josh asked. Before Tanya had a chance to reply, he'd left a lovely toothpastey smear across the screen. "Night-night, Grandma!"

Harriet's face wrinkled.

"That's disgusting!" The children all laughed as they trooped upstairs in their pyjamas.

"Night-night, Mum. Thanks for sharing the day with me."

Tanya and her mother smiled at each other across the miles.

"Thanks for inviting me – I wouldn't have missed it for the world." ■

Illustration by iStock.

# Push The Boundaries

## by Glenda Young

EY! Look at this!" Ann cried. "I think I've found exactly what I'm looking for."

She held up her new phone and waved it towards her husband, Mark.

"What is it, love?" he asked.

"It's a fishing group. They meet once a week down by the beach, weather permitting. It says here newcomers are welcome."

A smile spread across Ann's face.

"I think this could be just the thing I need to push me out of my comfort zone."

Mark, however, wasn't so sure.

"Fishing?" he teased. "You?"

"You don't think I can do it, don't you?" Ann said, rising to the challenge. "You never know, I might just ace it."

Ann made a note of the telephone number of the chap who ran the fishing group and planned to call him later that day.

Going fishing might never have been top of the list of pastimes back in the days when she was still working. But now Ann had taken voluntary redundancy, she had the freedom to try something new and make the most of her time.

"Are you sure about going fishing?" Mark asked. "I mean, why not choose a hobby that you're already good at?"

"It's all about challenging myself," Ann explained. "I want to do things I've never done before, have new experiences, meet new people and see the world through different eyes."

Mark smiled.

"Speaking of new experiences, how are you getting on with your new phone? Got to grips with it yet?"

Ann picked up the small booklet of instructions that came in the box with her new smartphone.

"I don't think I'll be needing this. I seemed to get the hang of it straight away."

\*     \*     \*     \*

A week later, Ann was ready to go fishing for the very first time. She checked the weather forecast and the day ahead looked sunny and warm.

It was a sea-fishing group she'd signed up for and she could hire a rod when she joined the group. She made up a lunch of sandwiches and fruit, threw on a T-shirt and jeans and set off for the walk to the beach.

She was greeted by the chap she'd spoken to on the phone but it didn't take her long to realise she was the only woman there.

Worse was to come, for when Ann tried to introduce herself to others in the group, she soon realised that not all of the fishermen were happy to have their space invaded by a woman.

Not one to be put off, and ready to accept the challenge she'd set herself, Ann settled down on the beach with the rod in her hand and a determined smile on her face.

She was shown how to attach the bait to the rod and how to cast into the sea. And then it was just a matter of waiting for a bite from a fish.

Ann waited . . . and she waited. She enjoyed sitting on the beach in the sun, watching the waves splash on the shore.

A cry went up along the shore. One of the men had caught something and she saw his rod bend into the waves as he pulled a large fish from the water.

Ann sat patiently, enjoying the peace and quiet and the sounds of the sea. She took out her lunch and ate it on the shingle beach.

But then the sky began to darken, and there was no mistaking the drops of rain that began to fall, leaving circles on the surface of the sea.

The men fishing alongside her pulled on anoraks and hats. They took cagoules from their backpacks and covered themselves to protect them from the rain.

Umbrellas went up but Ann had nothing except her sun hat to keep her dry and so she made her excuses and left. She walked home, trying to dodge the rain as best as she could.

"Catch anything?" Mark asked when he came in from work.

"Just a cold," Ann replied.

She took out her new phone and scrolled through websites, seeking more local activities on offer. After a day spent getting cold and wet with nothing to show for her efforts, she decided that perhaps fishing wasn't for her after all.

The next morning, when Mark was getting ready for work, Ann outlined her plans for the day.

"You're going to learn to play what?" He laughed.

"The ukulele," Ann said. "There's a group that meets twice a week, and they even provide the instruments. I found the group on my phone.

"They took a bit of discovering as they don't advertise themselves very well. But it says you don't need any experience to join.

"What's the worst that can happen? At least I'll be warm and dry indoors this time instead of getting soaked to my skin out fishing."

"But – the ukulele? Are you sure? You've never played any musical instrument before."

"Have faith in me, Mark." Ann smiled. "I want to do this. I want to push myself out of my . . ."

"Comfort zone, I know. And I admire you for it, love," he said. He kissed Ann and said goodbye before he drove off to his office in town.

\* \* \* \*

Later that day Ann set off for her local pub where the ukulele players were meeting. It was a friendly group she met there and, unlike the fishing group of the previous day, this time there were just as many women as men.

There were people of all ages, too, the younger ones being students, as she discovered when everyone introduced themselves.

Oh, yes, she thought. I'll be happy here.

Just then, Marie – the lady who ran the group – handed Ann a small wooden ukulele. Marie sat next to Ann and spent a few moments showing her how to hold the instrument.

Ann did her best to tuck it under her arm as Marie told her. Finally, she got the hang of holding it right. Then Marie separated Ann and another beginner from the main group of players and demonstrated how to pluck at the strings.

She explained the chords and how to auto-tune the instrument with a little digital device. Ann's head was spinning, but she was excited and willing to learn, to take in all the new information.

This was more like it. This was what she wanted. This was really

# My Superpower

There's something I find quite a puzzle,
Although I'm not one for complaining:
Whenever I hang out my washing,
As soon as my back's turned, it's raining!

In winter, with skies grey and heavy,
And icy winds starting to blow,
Inevitably – yes, the sun's out!
And I've promised the grandchildren snow!

I'm led to believe I've a talent –
A superpower, it would seem,
I think I'm directing the weather . . .
And so I've devised a good scheme!

For instance, if there's been a dry spell
And the garden is starting to roast,
I'll save myself starting to water
By planning a day at the coast!

I'm certain my ploy is now working,
I've definitely mastered the knack.
I'm off to the park with a picnic –
And I'm wearing my wellies and mac!

**Emma Canning.**

pushing her to learn something new and fun, too.

Ann placed her hands on the instrument as Marie had shown her. Her right hand was fine – she could pluck the strings and make a sound, if not exactly a joyous one yet. But she was determined to learn.

However, her left hand wouldn't do what everyone else's appeared to be doing with ease. Her wrist wouldn't twist around the neck of the ukulele, and her fingers weren't long enough to reach the strings there.

She tried harder but still couldn't do it without forcing her hand painfully around the neck of the ukulele. Marie saw Ann in difficulty and gently tried to encourage her fingers and wrist. But it was no good. Ann had to admit defeat.

\* \* \* \*

The next day, Ann told Mark that she was going to try something else, something more gentle, something she was sure that she could do.

"It's just yoga," she said. "I searched online and found a new class starting today. It's something I've never done before. It's just a bit of stretching, isn't it? How hard can it be?"

"Good luck with it," Mark said as he disappeared with a cheery wave.

After lunch that day, Ann set off for the church hall where the yoga class was being held. But instead of a bit of easy stretching, as she had imagined the yoga class might be, she was about to get an unwelcome surprise.

When she walked into the church hall the first thing that struck her was the heat. She wondered if the boiler was broken.

But no, it turned out that the yoga class she'd signed up for wasn't an easy stretching and breathing class. It was a hot yoga workout, and wasn't what Ann had hoped for at all.

Still, in the interests of doing something she'd never done before, Ann changed into her tracksuit bottoms, rolled out her yoga mat and claimed her space on the floor at the back of the hall.

She looked around and saw she was the eldest by far. The teacher at the front asked if anyone had any health problems she needed to be aware of.

Ann was just about to put up her hand and mention her stiff, painful fingers and her dodgy knee, but the teacher had moved on, encouraging the class to follow her in stretching to the right, to the left, to the floor and ceiling, and again, to the right, to the left . . .

Ann did her best, but she couldn't keep up with the hot speedy yoga. After ten minutes, she rolled up her mat and crept quietly away from the group.

\*    \*    \*    \*

"I don't know what I'm going to do, Mark," Ann said when her husband returned home from work that night. "Every time I try to do something new and out of my comfort zone, I don't seem to get it right."

"Maybe you should do something you're already good at," he suggested. "Take up your painting or sewing again?"

"But where's the challenge in that?" Ann sighed. She continued scrolling through a list of activity websites on her phone.

Just then Mark had an idea.

"You know the old library in town?"

"The one by your office? I thought it had closed down."

Mark nodded.

"When I went for a walk yesterday lunchtime, there was a notice on the window. They're reopening as a community library and they're looking for volunteers to help."

"But I don't know anything about libraries," Ann said.

"You know about researching to find activities. You know about finding your way around your new smartphone without the instruction manual.

"And with your background in teaching, you know you could help others to find places where they can learn new skills."

Ann thought for a moment and then shook her head.

"No, I couldn't possibly do that," she said.

Mark shot his wife a look.

"Not only could you do it, it's what you have been doing this week. You've done it without realising it. You've got skills you're not even aware of. I've been proud of you this week. You even went fishing, for heaven's sake."

"Fat lot of good it did me," Ann moaned.

"But you did it. You found the fishing group, just like you found the ukulele group and the yoga group, and I bet you've found a whole lot more activity groups on your phone since I came home from work."

Ann let her husband's words sink in.

"You're right," she said. "Learning how to use my new phone and finding all the groups online, I've been pushing myself out of my comfort zone without even realising it.

"I've been learning new skills all the time. Do you really think I could help other people do the same?"

Mark planted a kiss on Ann's cheek.

"I know you can," he said.

Ann made a note to call the community library first thing in the morning. Then she snuggled into Mark's side on the sofa. Now this was the kind of comfort zone she never wanted to leave. ■

WHEN rumours emerged of a Marx Brothers plan to spoof the 1942 classic "Casablanca", Warner Bros sent the Marx Brothers a warning letter. In typically witty style, Groucho responded in a well-publicised open letter.

"I just don't understand your attitude," he wrote. "Even if you plan on re-releasing the picture, I am sure that the average movie fan could learn in time to distinguish between Ingrid Bergman and Harpo. I don't know whether I could, but I certainly would like to try."

Groucho's manufactured spat with the studio ensured maximum publicity for "A Night In Casablanca". The film is a post-war comic mystery set in a hotel whose managers have an unfortunate habit of being murdered. The culprit, escaped Nazi war criminal Heinrich Stubel, aims to take over the hotel to access stolen treasure he has hidden there. Unfortunately for him, new manager Ronald Kornblow (Groucho) gleefully upsets guests and staff alike while dodging all Stubel's attempts to murder him.

The script delivers plenty of jokes and sight gags in one of the last of the Marx Brothers' major pictures together.

# Motive For Murder

## by Katie Ashmore

D ARLING, don't you just adore this shop?"
Ida smiled at her friend, Beatrice, and nodded.
"I do, Bea. The hampers it sells are heavenly."
"Yes, not to mention the chocolate and tea. But darling, are
you sure you haven't forgotten anything?"
Miss Ida Laverington and Miss Beatrice Fothersham had come to one
of the finest stores in London to order food for their planned expedition
to Hyde Park.

It was a warm October and they intended to go boating on the
Serpentine and enjoy a picnic with friends before winter set in.

Ida smiled.

"I don't think so, Bea," she told her, pulling on her gloves and placing
her cloche hat firmly over her smooth dark bob. "I've included the quail
and champagne. Can you think of anything I've left out?"

Beatrice arranged her fox fur and shook her head.

"Let's go and find Bates, then. I think he's parked the Bentley around
the corner."

They pressed the button for the lift and waited for it to rise to the
third floor. As the walnut doors slid apart, Ida looked expectantly for the
grinning face and berry uniform of the lift attendant.

However, he was nowhere to be seen. She pushed open the metal
grille herself, stepped inside and screamed.

"What's the matter, darling?" Beatrice, who was following closely
behind, stopped abruptly and gasped. "Goodness gracious!"

There, lying on the floor at their feet, was a body – a handsome young
man, his blue eyes staring at them, a bullet wound disfiguring his chest.

A dark stain was seeping through his jacket and his skin was as pale
as the store's marble walls.

Ida put her arm around Beatrice and escorted her swiftly back on to
the third floor.

"D-did you see, Ida? Darling, it – it was Ernest!"

*Illustration by iStock.*

Ida bit her lip and nodded.

"Try not to think about it, dear. We must find some brandy and telephone for the Constabulary."

\*    \*    \*    \*

The next day, the friends were still feeling shaken. They were sitting in the drawing-room of the Laveringtons' London home, taking tea and discussing events.

A pale sun shone through the large sash windows, lighting the flower display in the art deco fireplace and gleaming from the Tiffany lampshades.

Their friend Sir Francis Coursham was with them, as was Ida's mother, Lady Laverington. Ida took another sip of sweet tea and sighed.

"I still can't believe it," she declared. "Dear Ernest – dead. Murdered! It doesn't seem possible."

Francis nodded glumly and ate another cucumber sandwich.

"Such a decent chap," he said. He shook his head, lost for words.

Beatrice shuddered, and patted her Marcel wave.

"It was absolutely frightful, darlings. I'll never get that image out of my mind. Poor, sweet Ernest."

129

Mr Ernest Bonsham had been one of their set, a jolly good egg, and a guest invited on the proposed jaunt to Hyde Park. In point of fact, he had gone to the shop in search of the ladies to see if he could contribute to the provisions for that very occasion.

"It's frightful," Ida remarked. "Perhaps if he hadn't come in search of us, he'd still be alive." She blinked and bit her lip.

There was a moment's silence. Then Lady Laverington looked around at their dejected faces and rose to her feet.

"Enough of this," she said. "This won't bring Ernest back. Instead, why don't you set your minds on bringing the culprit to justice?"

She moved over to the sideboard and lifted the lid of a crystal decanter.

"I think you need something stronger than tea this afternoon. Now, drink this and solve the mystery."

Francis grinned and sat up straighter.

"I say, your mother's right. Let's find the bounder – for Ernest."

Beatrice twisted her string of beads in her long slim fingers.

"But where do we begin, darlings?" she asked.

"Don't you know anything about detective work?" Lady Laverington enquired, shaking her head. "Surely you've read Sir Arthur Conan Doyle or that wonderful new authoress, Agatha Christie?"

The young people regarded her with blank faces and she tutted.

"You need to consider motive and opportunity."

"Mummy, what are you talking about?"

Lady Laverington frowned at her daughter.

"Really, Ida. You young people should spend less time gadding about, drinking cocktails, and more time reading. What I mean is, why should someone want to kill Ernest? Who was there at the time?"

There was another moment's silence.

"Ernest was a total darling and terribly handsome. No-one would wish him harm," Beatrice said, her voice choked.

Ida patted her hand.

"Bea's right, Mummy. He was sweet and dreadfully popular."

Francis concurred, crossing his long legs and staring at the toes of his polished brogues.

"A top-notch fellow. I don't know what I'll do without him. Went to school together, fought in the trenches . . ." He swallowed, drank the rest of his brandy, then lit a cigarette.

Ida watched him with concern. He was a dapper young man, frightfully nice, and had been badly affected by the loss of his friend.

"Don't worry, Francis. We'll get to the bottom of this, whatever happens. Maybe it was the lift attendant? He had opportunity and it was awfully strange that he was nowhere to be seen when Bea and I found the body. Perhaps he ran away."

"Darling, I think you could be right. It was all very odd, but why would the attendant want to kill dear Ernest?"

"I say," Francis asked, "had either of you noticed any changes in Ernest? I thought he seemed himself, but you ladies are sometimes more observant about these things."

The girls thought for a moment, then shook their heads.

"I hadn't noticed any difference, darling," Beatrice remarked.

Then Ida had an idea.

"I hadn't, either, but let's ask Jessie. She saw him last."

\*     \*     \*     \*

The next afternoon, the Palms restaurant was busy. Waitresses in starched aprons and caps were moving amongst the crowds, serving thinly sliced sandwiches on silver trays and petits fours on gleaming cake stands.

Ida had called her friends together to see if they could get to the bottom of Ernest's murder.

Francis was sitting next to her, handsome in his cricket sweater and blue blazer, and Beatrice was opposite with their friend Miss Jessie Hurst-Smythe, who was the final member of the proposed Hyde Park trip.

"I say, do tell us how you got on, Ida. Did you speak to the constabulary?"

Ida looked up at Francis with large dark eyes.

"I did," she replied. "The inspector was awfully sweet, but they'd already questioned the lift boy and it wasn't him."

Beatrice seemed disappointed.

"How do they know, darling?"

"Apparently he has an alibi. He'd slipped away from his post for an assignation with one of the shop girls. I believe he's in quite some trouble with his employers."

"Serves him right." Beatrice pouted. "He should have been doing his job and taking care of Ernest."

Jessie patted her hand. She was a tall, striking girl with blonde hair and limpid blue eyes, but she was dreadfully scatty.

"Jessie, you saw him last. Did he seem himself?"

Jessie blinked at them.

"Did I?" she asked. "I suppose I must have done. The police said so, but I got rather confused when they questioned me."

Ida gritted her teeth and swallowed her impatience.

"Jessie dear, what do you remember? You saw Ernest on Wednesday." She nodded.

"Yes, I did," she replied. "Although I also went round on Friday, but the butler said he was out and . . ."

"Jessie!"

"Sorry. Yes, he seemed fine. I think we only talked about the boating trip. He was going to get some provisions for the picnic."

Ida sighed. Jessie would be no help after all.

"So, if it wasn't the lift attendant, who was it?" Beatrice asked, taking a salmon sandwich. "Where do we go from here?"

Ida thought for a moment.

"We need to discover who had a motive. Any ideas?"

Francis shook his head.

"I've been thinking about it a great deal and I can't think of anyone. He was an excellent fellow. Didn't have a single enemy."

Ida had to agree. It made no sense at all. Ernest was universally liked, so why should anyone murder him? Suddenly, inspiration struck.

"Goodness. What if it was a case of mistaken identity?"

Francis turned to her with a look of admiration.

"By Jove, you could be on to something. How terribly clever."

Ida blushed.

"Yes, but who could he have been mistaken for, darling?" Beatrice asked.

"It is terribly easy to muddle people up," Jessie commented. "I got myself in a rather embarrassing situation last autumn at the Wilford-Jones's ball. Do you remember, when I confused dear Ellen and Violet and . . ."

"That's it!" Francis's face was alight with excitement. "Ernest looked very like his brother, Cyril, didn't he?"

"Oh, yes, you're right." Ida was elated. Though two years apart in age, the young men had occasionally been mistaken for twins.

"What's this Cyril like, darlings? Would someone want to kill him?" Jessie giggled and Francis turned rather red.

"I'm afraid there's a number of people who might wish him harm," he remarked. "Cyril is the black sheep of the family. Great fun but always up to larks. Gets himself in frightful scrapes."

"Yes," Ida told her friend. "There are a number of young ladies or possibly their fathers . . . He could well owe some people money, too."

"Goodness." Beatrice raised one perfectly arched eyebrow. "I'd no idea that Ernest's family were so colourful."

There was a pause, then Ida spoke again.

"We ought to tell the police about this, as soon as possible. If Cyril's the target, he could still be in danger."

"I say, you're right. You are quick off the mark, Ida." Francis turned to gaze at her. "I'll drive you to the station directly."

\*    \*    \*    \*

The next day, the four friends were seated on a blanket on the banks of the Serpentine. To honour Ernest, they'd decided to go ahead with the picnic.

The leaves of the chestnut trees had turned scarlet and gold. A squirrel scampered up the trunk of a lime, an acorn clamped firmly in his mouth.

Ida raised her glass of champagne.

"To Ernest!" she said.

"Ernest!" the others chorused.

"What about Cyril?" Jessie asked. "Is he still alive?"

"I believe he's perfectly well. The constabulary are keeping an eye on him, while they carry out enquiries."

"He may be the black sheep," Beatrice remarked, "but I feel terribly sorry for him. Imagine – how frightful to be stalked by a murderer!"

Ida nodded.

"It must be terrifying. Do they have any leads yet?"

Francis shook his head. He looked particularly handsome today, Ida thought, in his rowing whites and navy jumper.

"I don't believe they've had much luck. Seems his father paid off all his debts quite recently and he's been steering clear of the fairer sex since he was almost trapped into matrimony by a most unsuitable woman."

Ida sighed.

"Oh, dear, we don't seem much further forward, do we?"

"Never mind, darling. Let's enjoy our picnic. Then we can turn our minds to business."

They opened the hampers, exclaiming over the delicacies inside. They partook of quail and cold chicken, Scotch eggs and soft white rolls, Waldorf salad and the most delightful lemon syllabub.

"I say, I think we should do this every day," Francis remarked with satisfaction, as they finished their repast.

There was silence.

"Well," Beatrice said, at last. "If the constabulary can't find anyone who wants to kill Cyril, maybe Ernest was the intended victim, after all."

The others looked at her.

"I don't know, Bea. What's the motive? Ernest was such a darling."

"Maybe there's something we don't know about. Something from his past. What do you think, Francis? You knew him best."

Francis frowned.

"He's always been a jolly good chap. Well-liked. Honourable." He paused, then shook his head. "There was a situation in France – in the war – but no, not worth mentioning . . ."

Ida shrugged and rose to her feet.

"Shall we go on our rowing trip then, before it turns colder?" she asked. "I don't think we'll get much further with our detective work today."

"Good idea," Francis replied, standing and dusting crumbs from his trouser legs. "Whatever the truth, at least we know Cyril will be safe. There's a policeman guarding the front of his house."

Jessie giggled.

"Everyone seems to have people outside their homes," she remarked.

"Darling, what are you talking about?"

"Ernest. Ernest had someone outside his house." She smiled round at them and nodded her head.

"Ernest had someone hanging around outside his house?" Francis demanded. "When? Who? Why on earth didn't you say, Jessie?"

"Oh, do you think it might be important?"

Francis groaned and Beatrice tutted with impatience.

"Yes, dear," Ida told her. "When did you see the person and what did they look like?"

"It was a woman. I spoke to her."

"You spoke to her! For goodness' sake, Jessie, tell us before I shake it out of you."

"It was on Friday, when I went to call on Ernest, but the butler said he was out. I told you, remember? Well, I'd just come down the steps, when a woman stopped me and asked if Ernest Bonsham lived there. I told her he did, but was out. That was all."

"What was this woman like?"

"She was short, dark, with an accent – French, perhaps?"

Francis gasped and blanched.

"A French woman," he stuttered. "It can't be."

"What is it, Francis, dear?"

He swallowed.

"I think you may have met the murderess, Jessie," he announced.

\*　\*　\*　\*

A few days later, Ida and Francis were out for dinner. The restaurant was busy, filled with laughter and tantalising scents, and the soft tones of a jazz band floated from the corner.

"You were so clever to figure it out, Francis," Ida told him. "Thanks to you, Ernest has justice."

Francis reddened and shook his head.

"Oh, no. I'd never have done it without your ideas." He smiled. "You've been simply marvellous."

A French woman, Marie Lafontelle, had been arrested two days before. It had transpired that while fighting in France, Ernest – believing he would die in the next offensive and somewhat under the influence – had met and married Marie in the space of a week.

Unbeknown to him, she was with child, and when he didn't return, she had nursed resentment for several years. Recently, their little boy had died of measles and, unhinged by grief, she had come to seek revenge.

"The tragedy is that, if poor Ernest had known any of this, I'm sure he would have stood by her. He was such a top-rate fellow."

"Yes, but surely he knew he had a wife."

Francis shook his head sadly.

"He received a head injury at the battle of Ypres and those six months were a blank to him ever after."

Ida stared in amazement.

"Why didn't one of his friends tell him?" she asked.

Francis rubbed his forehead, his face scarlet.

"We should have done, but none of us knew about the child. We all thought it best to leave well alone. His family would never have approved of the liaison. It was done in a moment of madness and Ernest remembered nothing about it."

"How sad." Ida sighed. "Poor Marie. Poor Ernest."

Francis looked at her and took her hand.

"You're far too beautiful to be glum," he said. "And Ernest wouldn't want us to be miserable, so I think you'd better dance with me."

Ida smiled, her sadness forgotten.

"I expect you're right," she said. "Let's dance." ■

ALAN LADD and Veronica Lake starred in their third pairing in novelist Raymond Chandler's first original screenplay. The melodrama follows the story of returning bomber pilot Johnny Morrison, who discovers that during his absence, his wife, Helen, has been having an affair with Eddie Harwood, owner of the Blue Dahlia nightclub. Worse, during a row, Helen confesses that their young son did not die of diphtheria, as she had led Johnny to believe, but as the result of her own drunken driving. They fight and Johnny leaves.

Later, after being discarded by Eddie, Helen is murdered with Johnny's gun and Johnny is suspected of the killing. Proving his innocence is no easy matter.

Though successful, the film had a troubled journey to the cinemas. Chandler, already a popular writer, had only partly written his screenplay when filming began. The studio found itself in the uncomfortable position of running out of script, and had to grant Chandler the rare privilege of writing at home to finish it.

Despite its challenging start, the film was nominated for an Oscar for best original screenplay.

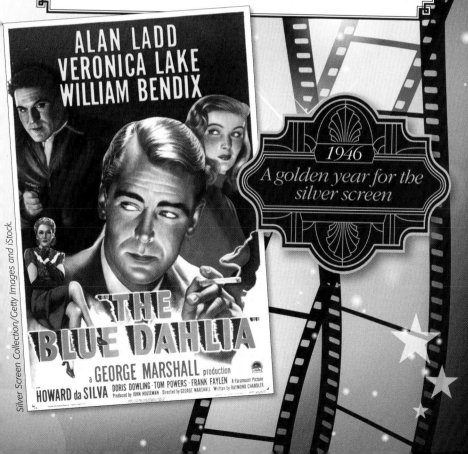

1946

*A golden year for the silver screen*

# Up In Smoke

## by Patricia Belford

SASHA always felt a shiver of excitement every time she turned the corner into Church View. It was six weeks since she and Ross had moved into Number Seven.

They still relished the thrill of knowing that, after several years of saving for a deposit, they had finally found a house they could afford.

Just in time, for they were expecting their first baby in May. She wondered if she could persuade Ross to agree to have a trip to town at the weekend to have a look round at baby equipment.

Her parents, delighted at the prospect of the arrival of their first grandchild, had offered to buy a cot and a pushchair.

Sasha reached the gate of their modest semi-detached house. The front garden was tidy and colourful with Michaelmas daisies flowering under the window and a scattering of gold and bronze beech leaves on the lawn.

Luckily, the long back garden, which was neglected and overgrown, could not be seen from the street. One day, they would get around to tackling the weeds.

First, though, they had to put the house in order. Over the last few weekends, and often in the evenings, as well, they had painted their bedroom and the kitchen.

It was hard work, but they had had fun doing it together. The next project would be the nursery, and Sasha was already dreaming up colour schemes for it.

Today, Ross had taken a couple of days' leave from the office in order to lay the vinyl on the sitting-room floor.

A sofa, grey to tone with the striped curtains, was due to be delivered next week. Sasha had sewn cushion covers in a beautiful floral design of graphite, pink and lime green and Ross had renovated and polished an old coffee table which they had bought in a charity shop.

It was all going to look wonderful. She couldn't wait to see the new floor.

"Hi, love, I'm home!"

She closed the front door and hung her jacket on one of the pegs in the hall. As she stepped forward her foot caught on something and she was startled to see two empty beer bottles roll across the floor.

"I'm in here, Sasha!"

*Illustration by Ruth Blair.*

"Sorry, I'm late. The traffic was down to a crawl and the bus took ages. Oh!"

Sasha stood at the door, shocked. She had been expecting to admire a shining floor laid with pale pine-effect vinyl. Instead, most of the sitting-room floor was missing.

Ross was sitting on one of the few remaining floorboards with his feet in a huge gaping hole. His face was grim.

"What's happened? Why have you taken the floorboards up?"

"It's bad news, love. I'm sorry."

"What do you mean?"

"We've got dry rot. The whole sitting-room floor – the joists, too."

Sasha gasped.

"Are you sure?"

Ross nodded.

"Quite sure. I stuck a screwdriver in and the wood just crumbled. I had to get Charlie to come . . ."

"So that's why those beer bottles are lying about in the hall. I might have guessed Charlie had been round!"

"Hang on, love, he came to lend a hand, give me some moral support. Besides, it's a two-man job, taking up floorboards," Ross said. "I just

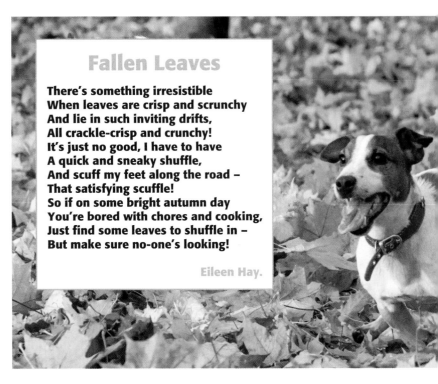

## Fallen Leaves

There's something irresistible
When leaves are crisp and scrunchy
And lie in such inviting drifts,
All crackle-crisp and crunchy!
It's just no good, I have to have
A quick and sneaky shuffle,
And scuff my feet along the road –
That satisfying scuffle!
So if on some bright autumn day
You're bored with chores and cooking,
Just find some leaves to shuffle in –
But make sure no-one's looking!

Eileen Hay.

forgot to take the bottles out to the recycling bin."

"It doesn't matter," Sasha said, stepping cautiously into the room.

She sank down on to the floor beside Ross, then shuddered as she saw the rough, stony foundations of the house under the floor, below the joists.

"The surveyor should have spotted it and mentioned it in his report," Ross said. "We'll have to speak to him."

"What are we going to do? We've no spare cash. How can we afford to have a joiner in to fit new floorboards?"

"I've worked it all out," Ross said, holding up an envelope. "We'll do it ourselves, me and Charlie, at weekends."

Sasha sighed.

"Wonderful. I suppose we can look forward to weeks of sawing and hammering and mess," she said. "Not to mention Charlie drinking beer and banging on about Manchester United!"

"We won't be drinking beer while we're handling power tools," Ross said. "And Charlie's a good bloke. I couldn't have managed without him today.

"For goodness' sake, love, how do you think I felt when I realised it was dry rot?"

Sasha felt her eyes filling.

"I'm sorry, Ross, don't let's quarrel. I do understand. I came home

expecting to see the new floor laid. It was such a shock."

"For me, too. I'm still reeling. I knew the house needed a lot of work but I never expected anything like this.

"And I've been miserable all day, dreading having to break the news to you."

Sasha tried to brush away her tears with the back of her hand.

"It's not your fault. But money is so tight." She gasped. "I've just remembered the party. We'll have to cancel it!"

They had planned to combine their house-warming party with a celebration for Ross's father's sixtieth birthday. Sasha's parents, who had recently retired to Portugal, would be coming over for it.

"And Mum rang, during the lunch break. They've booked their flights, so they will be here the day before, well . . . before the party would have been."

Ross shook his head.

"They'll understand. We'll have to have the party later. We can ask them to change their booking. And my dad's not much of a party man, anyway, so he won't mind."

Sasha reached for Ross's hand.

"When we first came to view the house, the estate agent said it had unique features.

"I thought he meant the stained-glass windows in the hall, but nothing could be more unique than a sitting-room without a floor!"

Suddenly, they were both laughing. Perched on the creaking board near the door, they hugged. Ross heaved himself to his feet.

"Come on, love, I can't do anything more tonight. It's a bad situation but you've cheered me up. We'll get through it somehow."

"I think you need a shower. You've got sawdust in your hair and cobwebs on your sweater," Sasha said.

"And you, dear Sasha, have some rather fetching dirty streaks on your nose!"

"You get off upstairs. I'll wash my face in the kitchen sink and then start the tea. I've bought some of those sausages you like."

"Great. With baked beans and chips?"

"No chips. They're bad for you. I'll do jacket potatoes instead."

Sasha switched on the oven. As she began to scrub the potatoes, she thought how thankful she was that they hadn't booked that holiday in Cyprus they'd fancied.

She wondered how much the new floorboards would cost.

Charlie had some useful contacts and would know the best place to go to buy wood but even with his help they would be struggling to meet the expense of a whole new floor.

She wished she hadn't moaned about Charlie. He and Ross went back a long way and Charlie was a good friend to them both.

A big, untidy man with a loud voice, he was obsessed with football, but he was kind and loyal. Sasha resolved to try not to criticise him in future.

Maybe they could ask him to be the baby's godfather. He would be sure to want to teach the child to kick a ball, even if it was a girl.

She was grinning as she turned the sausages when Ross joined her.

"Something smells good. What's the joke?"

"I was thinking we should ask Charlie to be our baby's godfather."

"He'll be thrilled! Probably give it a Man U scarf for a christening present!"

Chuckling, Ross fetched the tomato ketchup from the cupboard.

"The sausages and jacket spuds have given me a great idea. We can make the best of a bad situation."

Sasha paused, spatula in hand.

"What do you mean?"

"I know what we can do with those floorboards. There's plenty of space in the back garden. We'll pile 'em up at the far end and invite everyone round for the party!"

"Party?"

"Yes. Your mum and dad won't have to change their flights. It's November the fifth in three weeks, a perfect time to get rid of all that rotten wood.

"We'll cook masses of sausages and jacket potatoes, get some drinks in and buy a few fireworks and sparklers.

"Charlie can be in charge of the fireworks. It'll be a housewarming in more ways than one. We'll have a bonfire party!" ■

# Fountains Abbey, Yorkshire

This monastery, situated near Ripon, was once the wealthiest in England until Henry VIII put paid to that with the Dissolution in 1539. Stone from the Abbey was then used to construct local buildings, including Fountains Hall, and the monastic ruins by the River Skell are now the largest and most complete example in the country.

Founded back in 1132, the Abbey had been home to hundreds of Cistercian monks and lay brothers, and the area was ideal for sheep farming, bringing wealth to the Abbey. As the name suggests, Fountains Abbey came from the springs in the area.

The sheer scale of Fountains Abbey is breathtaking. It sits in the grounds of Studley Royal Estate, which is home to a variety of wildlife including birds and deer. Owned by the National Trust, the Abbey ruins, along with the 18th-century water garden, are a dramatic spectacle and a great day out.

Little wonder, then, that the World Heritage Site is visited by more than 400,000 visitors annually.

# The Waterlily Girls

## by Em Barnard

ONE lazy August afternoon, four young friends walked into the countryside surrounding their village, eager to pursue their love of nature through fresh surroundings. Ann had her Kodak, Jo her sketchpad, Stella and Nicola notepads. After a few shots across the fields, Ann broke from the pack and raced down a bridlepath.

Her three friends dashed after her and they fell, giggling, against a five-bar gate, breathless from the sprint. Ann pointed.

"See? Told you there's a flower meadow behind this cabbage field."

She raced on down the lane against a cheering accompaniment from birds in the hedgerows. The others followed, all ignoring a weather-worn straw bale which had been tossed against the hedgerow. Gripped under its two binding twines was a grubby board marked *PRIVATE*.

Moments later the girls were leaning over another gate, gazing across a meadow of wavering grasses speckled with dazzling wildflowers.

Ann began snapping away with her camera. Her dad was a wildlife photographer and Ann yearned to follow in his footsteps. Jo began a pencil drawing as an outline for her pastel art. Stella and Nicola jotted notes on their pads.

"Oi, you lot!" An elderly farmer appeared from the hedgerow behind them. They sprang back, grouping together. "What are you up to? You shouldn't be down this track. It's signed well enough. Now, off you go." He flapped a hand.

Ann pointed at the meadow.

"Couldn't we go in just for a few minutes? We'd stay on the verge. You see, I want to be a nature photographer." She held up her camera.

"I want to be a flower artist." Jo showed her sketch of red campions. Stella supported them.

"I want to be a biologist. I'm interested in insects and birds."

His eyes darted to Nicola, who was gripping her pad tight against her top. Ann knew how shy she was, and that her dream was to write fiction. In the hope he'd grant their wish, Ann decided to answer for her.

"She likes writing stories about animals."

The farmer glanced at each of them.

"Well, there's dangerous machinery up and down here and I don't want any kids getting hurt. Now skedaddle."

The following evening, camera at her eye, Ann was again standing on the lower bar of the gate to the meadow. The descending sun was flooding a peach hue over it and she was getting some great shots. Jo had her pad on the top rail, sketching.

Ann lowered her camera and looked about. There was no sound of machinery. They'd seen no-one along the lane. She stepped down and tugged the bolt back.

"Ann, no. If we get caught . . ." Stella stretched to grab her, but Ann slipped through with a giggle. She began snapping the vibrant flowers and the congregation of butterflies and insects feeding on them.

Then, spotting the others approaching, she ran on to the far end of the meadow where it slipped into a copse of trees.

She stopped by a tree trunk, waiting till her friends topped the rise. She stepped out into squelching grassland which dipped to a dark pool of scummy water.

"Yuk. Is that a pond or a bog?" Jo asked, as she and the other two arrived beside her. It was dank and still.

But Ann had spotted life further down, a lone yellow star-like flower reaching above the scum beside yellowing plate-like leaves – a waterlily. Determined to snap it, or even recover it, she kicked off her shoes and socks.

"I'm not going down there in these sandals," Nicola said, wrinkling her nose.

"Ann, don't, it's too dodgy." Stella caught her arm.

Ann tugged free and, clutching her camera, waded through the dishevelled grasses, her feet sucking in the soft mud. She'd set a cautious foot between the reeds and had sunk up to her calves until . . .

"Help me! Help me!"

The girls stopped.

"Over here! I'm trapped!"

Ann was already stepping out, her legs speckled with slime. Dipping under the feathery willows, she stopped in amazement. A blue tractor sat with its front wheels deep in the bog.

"Where are you?" she called.

"Over here. Keep to the high bank!" he yelled.

Ann climbed to where it seemed the tractor must have rolled down. Stepping along the rise and to the far side, she spotted the farmer in a crumpled old jacket, up to his thighs in the bog beside the front tyre, clutching at the grassy bank.

"How can we help you?"

"Stay there! Go back the way you came and go to the farm. It's across the lane and over the rise. Tell Joe in the cottage opposite what's happened, and to bring the digger and chains to the old pond!"

Ann stumbled back to the others and told them what to do. As they scuttled off she gave her camera to Stella, telling her she was staying with the old man.

From the rise Ann gaped as the tractor shifted slightly. She slid down the grassy bank. His eyes were closed, his breathing hard.

His face was streaked with mud and red with sweat and effort, and Ann took out her hanky and smoothed it over his muddy brow. He opened his eyes and looked at her, surprised.

"Why, you're one of those girls from yesterday."

"I'm sorry we've trespassed. It was my idea. Are you hurt badly?"

"Foot's pinned under the wheel. Nothing broken, thanks to the mud. I've been avoiding this place since my wife died some years back. We used to picnic here, when it was pretty.

"Then someone dumped some chemical in it so I came to see about filling it in. I went to get out of the tractor and caught the gear lever in this old jacket, and next I'm hanging out the side and, well . . . that was a good hour ago. Then the tractor died so here we lay.

"Was what you said true, or were you just playing me up about your ambitions so I'd give you permission to go on the wildflower meadow?"

"Yes, it's all true. 'Cept Nicola. She wants to write romances. But we wouldn't have picked the flowers, and we kept to the headland just now when we came through."

"Well, you can now see why I wouldn't let you on it. Too close to here, too dangerous."

Ann turned her hanky to a clean spot.

"I wanted to get to the yellow waterlily. It'll die in there, like all the others. Can't you save it, and the pond?" She wiped mud from his cheek. "Then you could have your picnics here again."

"No, it's never held the same joy for me since Cissy went. We never had kids, so I'm alone now. What's your name?"

"Ann Drake. I live up Foxhall Road."

"I'm Tom Jackson. Now, Ann, it's getting dark. Go to the rise and wait for Joe. Then go back to the lane and home, all of you. I don't want you around machinery, getting hurt, too.

"And look at the state of you. Your parents won't be happy about any of this."

So Ann found out as she stepped through the kitchen door. Her dad stopped eating his supper.

"Where've you been till this late hour?"

Her mum turned from the sink and hurried to her side.

"What happened?"

"I'm all right," Ann said brightly. "I – we saved a farmer who got hurt. We heard him when we were down near his pond. His tractor –"

"Pond? Where was this?"

"On his farm, Dad. But we were only taking photos," she said as her mum tutted at the state of her. "I was trying to take a photo of a waterlily and . . ."

"Let's get you in a bath," her mum said, hurrying her out of her dad's firing range.

"I'll take that." Her dad held a hand out and Ann reluctantly placed her camera in it.

The following morning, Saturday, Ann met the others in town. They'd all been truthful, sure their parents would be proud of them, but they had all suffered rebukes regarding trespassing.

"I wanted to take him some flowers," Ann said. "It only seems . . . caring to ask after him. But I've another plan."

There was a groan of protest from the others, who thought it would be better to forget the whole affair.

"We could make our own get-well card. We could post it. Jo could do a coloured pastel of what the pond would look like done up.

"And Nicola could write a story about it, say through the eyes of the insects that live there."

"If my dad—" Nicola began.

"Stella will help you with the insects. Then — you'll like this bit. We sign ourselves —"

"No!" Nicola cried. "If my dad finds I've had anything more to do with it all he'll kill me." The other two nodded in agreement.

"I was going to say," Ann went on, "we sign ourselves, 'the Waterlily Girls.' You're always taking about pen names, Nicola."

"So that's why you wanted me to bring my pastels." Jo tossed her pad and pastel stick on the grass. Ann looked at Stella, who returned her gaze sceptically.

But soon, the other two gave in. Knowing her insects, Stella helped Nicola with the story. Jo's pastels flowed effortlessly, using the pond before her for inspiration.

As she didn't have her camera, Ann gave instructions for the best effects, especially the pond's massing pink and white waterlilies. By the time they wandered home early evening, they were chatting and laughing, eager to complete and post it.

The following Saturday, Ann burst through the garden gate with a clutch of library books.

"Hi, Dad," she called, catching sight of him in the doorway of his shed.

"Hold on, I want a word with you, young lady."

As she stepped inside she spotted the envelope on his bench.

"Yes, you know what that is, don't you? Mr Jackson brought it round this morning. He wanted to thank you in person. Ann, I felt a fool, embarrassed that I knew nothing about it.

"Just tell me in future, like you did last time. I shall show this to your friends' parents so they know, too. Then I'll take it back to Mr Jackson as he'd like to keep it. Now off you go."

It was worth the telling-off. Ann now knew Mr Jackson had received the card and that he was well enough to come round and thank them.

But it had thwarted her hopes of speaking to her dad regarding another plan she'd conceived. It would have to wait till he'd forgotten this affair.

\* \* \* \*

A month later, the affair with the card was forgotten, though her three friends had, strangely, not received a further rebuke or any mention of it from their parents.

So it was time, they agreed, to allow Ann to broach their new plan to her dad. It burst from her one Sunday, during lunch.

"Dad, can we have a pond in our garden?" He continued eating. "Oh, Dad, please. We're the only ones that have a garden big enough.

"And we've been reading up on ponds from library books. You see, you have to make sure the sand beneath the liner is dead smooth so stones don't tear it, and you have to have different depths.

"Waterlilies like it deepish, and flag iris and marsh marigolds prefer the shallow margins. And you need oxygenating plants to make sure all the wildlife thrives. Oh, and grass, not stones, round the edge so baby frogs can climb out and hedgehogs can drink safely. And . . ."

"All right! I get the message."

"Oh, Dad, thanks. When can we start?"

As well as giving his approval, he persuaded the other parents to help, convinced this project would keep their girls close to home.

The girls themselves, eager to begin, worked to clear the plot of stones and weeds. Parents popped round whenever they could, and by the end of November the pond was ready.

Green shoots were sprouting by the first of March, the day for planting up. Everyone bought plants to suit it. Stella, Jo and Nicola brought waterlilies, each a different colour. Ann's were yellow, of course.

Patiently they waited for the summer for the plot to erupt with colour, and the pond to sparkle and shine with its water plants and wildlife.

When the first waterlily bud burst open, a celebration took place around the pond. Once filled with cake and contentment, Ann's dad passed her an envelope. Ann stared at it.

"It's addressed to the Waterlily Girls." She flashed a look to the other three. Ann opened it and read out the words inside.

"'I hope you have an enjoyable party. Your dad will explain why I'm getting in touch after all this time. Best regards, Tom Jackson.'"

Ann looked at her dad.

"Come on." He smiled and marched towards the house. The adults left behind smiled knowingly.

\*    \*    \*    \*

Half an hour later, Dad drove the girls up the drive to Tom's house. He stepped out to meet them.

"My goodness, look how you've grown," he said cheerily, looking from one to the other. The girls tried a smile, still puzzled. "Hop in my old Ford estate and I'll take you for a ride around the farm."

His direction was away from the old pond the girls presumed he'd restored.

"No, after that accident I filled it in," he told them. "Meadow's still there."

Minutes later he pulled up beside a high hedge. He took them through a gate into a sloping meadow massed with wildflowers.

The girls stared, open-mouthed, squeezing each other in glee as he led them through it to a shining new pond, cobalt blue in the sunshine.

Reeds and marginals ringed it like a fertile crown. Water boatmen and whirligig beetles skated on its surface, sending glittering ripples across it.

Songbirds, insects and butterflies fluttered above, rejoicing in their new-found habitat. Joy was expressed on the girls' faces, too.

"It was your card that did it. Your care and concern not just for me but for the wildlife conveyed in the little story. It gave me the incentive to try to replicate it."

"Look at the waterlilies," Stella said, gripping Ann's hand in delight.

"Pink, white, and yellow just like ours."

Tom scratched his bristled chin.

"I dug that other yellow one out of the bog, and it's thriving in a barrel pond in my back garden. You're welcome any time. Picnics, whatever."

"And you must come and see our pond . . ." Ann gave her dad a sheepish glance, wondering if he'd agree to that.

He smiled.

"Tom's welcome any time."

\*　\*　\*　\*

During visits home through school and university years, they'd congregate by the pond in Ann's garden or by Tom's pond, often with him. Tom became a firm friend.

The meadows and ponds became inspirational for the girls as university sent them onward to pursue their dreams.

They'd made a pact to meet up the summer they turned twenty-five. When Ann arrived home for the reunion, her dad told her some startling news regarding Tom's farm.

"Compulsory purchase!" Ann sat down, shocked.

"They want to build further houses on his land."

"But they can't. What about the wildflower meadows? And the pond?"

"Tom's already sold it. He's tired, Ann."

Ann was worried for him as she waited at his door.

"Ann!" Smiling, eyes gleaming, Tom took her hand. "Come in."

"Tom, why didn't you tell us? We could have helped you fight this."

"Ann, you can't win against authority. I've had the best years of my life here but it's never been the same since Cissy died."

"But where will you go?"

"I'm moving to Torquay, close to my sister Daphne. All that British Riviera sun, eh?" A mischievous twinkle lit his eyes.

Emotion gripped her.

"So will they . . ." She bit back her words. It seemed callous to mention the meadow and pond.

"Yes, Ann, they will bulldoze it all. Now don't get upset." He patted her hand. "I've bought ten acres from my pal at Willow Cross farm, a few miles north of where you live.

"I want you four girls to have it.

"No, listen. I owe you girls my life," he insisted. "If I'd been stuck out there all that night, I wouldn't be here now. And I wouldn't have had all these lovely years with you all.

"Trouble is . . . it's a bit boggy, this patch of land," he said, a twinkle in his eyes.

Ann caught on.

"What you mean is, it would made a fine place for a pond, maybe some wildflowers, a habitat for insects. Somewhere to picnic."

He nodded. Ann hugged him, delighted.

"We're all going to have the best celebration ever, round the garden pond this evening. You will come, won't you?" ■

**W**ORLD WAR II was a recent memory when Powell and Pressburger's "A Matter Of Life And Death" received its premiere at the first-ever Royal Film Performance on November 1, 1946.

Retitled "Stairway To Heaven" in America, the film opens with plucky RAF pilot Peter Chapman (David Niven) in a seemingly hopeless attempt to land his blazing Lancaster bomber, guided by American radio operator June (Kim Hunter). Despite having no parachute, he finally jumps out of the doomed plane.

A heavenly administrative mix-up leaves our hero still in one piece – but now he's falling in love with that unseen American girl whose voice helped him through those "final" moments.

Arriving to accompany the doomed pilot into the afterlife, Conductor 71 (Marius Goring) must return empty-handed. Justice demands that the case be tried in a celestial court, where fate and love lie in the balance.

Celebrated for its visual effects – Technicolor scenes on Earth contrast with a pearly monochrome afterlife, and that iconic stairway to heaven – the philosophical fantasy was a hit with post-war cinemagoers, and remains a firm favourite today.

1946

*A golden year for the silver screen*

GAUMONT-EAGLE-LION
Une production of The Archers

A MATTER
of LIFE
and DEATH

Une Question
de Vie et de Mort

David **NIVEN**   Kim **HUNTER**
Roger **LIVESEY**   Raymond **MASSEY**

Production et Mise en scène MICHAEL POWELL et EMERIC PRESSBURGER
"Een Zaak on Leven en Dood"

# On The Inside

## by Alyson Hilbourne

G O and get into bed and I'll read a story."
Sophie skipped off as Fiona pulled the plug from the bath and
swished away the tidemark. Then she hung up the towels and
followed Sophie down the hall to her bedroom.
"Which story tonight?"
"The one about families."

Fiona smiled but inwardly she sighed. Ever since discovering the story,
Sophie had chosen the book to be read several times a week. She also
looked at the pictures on her own.

The result was that the book looked as it if had been hauled around
the world in all sorts of weather rather than sitting in a suburban
bedroom. The spine was broken, some of the pages were torn and
others were smudged and stained.

"Night, darling," Fiona said when she'd finished reading. She leaned
down to give Sophie a kiss.

"Mummy?" Sophie propped herself up on an elbow. "Mr Hargreaves
says there is going to be a pet show at the school fair. Can I take
Buggles?"

At the sound of his name Buggles came hopping upstairs and nosed
open the door to Sophie's room.

"Buggles!" Fiona said. "You know you're not allowed upstairs."

Buggles sank to the floor and made himself as flat as possible as
Sophie laughed and clapped her hands.

Fiona smiled. The dog was a character. When Mike had walked out on
them they had gone to the rescue centre and chosen him to help fill the
gap left in their lives, and he had certainly done that.

He wasn't big, was of very mixed parentage and would, Fiona guessed,
be an excellent ratter. As it was he used his skills to seek out food,
finding chip papers, fast food bags and crisp wrappers whenever they
were out, and stealing any food in the house that wasn't put away.

The result was that he was quite rotund and his eyes were even more

bug-like than when they'd got him. If awards were given for the least attractive dog ever he'd have been a contender, but Fiona and Sophie loved him to bits.

"A pet show, eh?" Fiona scratched the dog's ears. "I expect so. Now, goodnight, Sophie. Buggles – downstairs!"

The entry form for the pet show came home from school the following week and Fiona helped Sophie fill it in. Sophie spent extra time brushing Buggles and trying to train him to sit and stand to order.

"Kieran is going to come to the fair tomorrow," Fiona said on Friday evening.

Sophie scowled.

Fiona ignored her and tried to still the unease in her stomach. She would really have liked Sophie to get along with Kieran. So far she had met him twice and each time she'd been unfriendly and standoffish, very unlike her usual ebullient self.

Fiona wasn't sure why Sophie had taken such a dislike to him. It couldn't be because she was worried he'd replace her father, who had shown no interest in Sophie since he'd remarried.

But Fiona kept quiet and pressed her lips together. She'd done her best to conduct her relationship with Kieran out of Sophie's sight and, apart from two evenings when her mother had babysat, she'd met him for lunches and coffees when Sophie was at school.

Fiona wanted to see him more often but Sophie's icy attitude was keeping them apart for now.

The school fair and pet show should be a good environment for them to mix, but it seemed Sophie was not going to make it easy.

Next morning Sophie was frantically brushing Buggles.

"How does he look?"

There was a knock at the door and she got up to let Kieran in.

"Hello, Sophie," he greeted her. "Looking forward to this?"

Sophie was non-committal and Fiona shrugged apologetically. Kieran smiled. They put Buggles on his lead and walked to school.

In the hall, long tables had been set up for the various cages, tanks and bowls. Anxious children hovered near their pets, some fussing and making last-minute adjustments, while others were obviously itching to get outside and explore the rest of the fair.

"What are those?" Sophie bent down to peer into a large glass tank. "Those tortoises are swimming!"

"They're terrapins," Kieran said. "They can go in water or on land."

In the next tank a large snake was coiled round on itself rather like a Cumberland sausage. Most of the cages contained cats, some relaxed and lying down, others frantic to get out and hissing as people passed by.

"Shall we take a look round the rest of the fair?" Kieran asked.

"No, I want to stay here. I don't want to miss anything." Sophie's mouth was pressed into a sullen line.

Fiona checked the schedule.

"It's OK, Sophie. They'll judge the pets here first, then the dogs outside. We've plenty of time. I'll make sure we don't miss anything." She kept her voice light.

Sophie was persuaded outside but she made a show of dragging her feet as they went. They walked around the stalls.

"Would you like to have a go at fishing for ducks, Sophie? Or try the coconut shy?" Kieran rattled the coins in his pocket. Fiona felt a rush of warmth for him. He was trying so hard.

Sophie shook her head.

At the second-hand book stall Kieran bought a couple of paperbacks, and then a plate of samosas from Mrs Singh at the next stall.

"Would you like one?" Kieran offered Sophie the plate.

Sophie's lip curled and Fiona felt her body tense. She really wanted to haul Sophie off home, but making a show would be embarrassing for all of them. Instead, she gave Kieran an apologetic smile.

"I'd like one, please!"

She knew Sophie feared losing her mum to Kieran, but of course that would never happen. She would always be her number one priority. Fiona found herself being pulled in different directions and it was leaving her stretched and taut.

"Will everyone please bring their dogs to the judging ring!" The Tannoy called them back to the judging area.

"He might not win," Fiona warned as Sophie prepared to take Buggles into the field. "There are lots of pets here."

Sophie flicked her hair back.

"But Buggles is the best."

"I've a feeling she might be disappointed," Fiona said to Kieran as they watched Sophie stand in line and try to persuade Buggles to sit at her feet.

Two judges in white coats with clipboards walked up and down the row of children and dogs. They stopped, spoke to each child and patted the dogs. Then they went off to consult and Sophie wandered back.

A short while later the Tannoy crackled into life again. A man with a microphone stood in the centre of the field. The judges stood next to him with a clutch of rosettes in their hands.

"Ladies, gentlemen and students. The results of the pet show. Please know that the judges found it a very difficult decision and wished they could have given everyone a prize." He cleared his throat. "But, to begin. In fourth place is Jonathan with his pet, Freddie."

A blond boy clutching a large tortoise ran up to the judges. They handed him a green rosette.

"A tortoise? You can't love that!" Sophie was scornful.

"In third place is Ruby with her pet, Pickles."

An older girl walked over with a small dog on a lead. The dog was dressed in a skirt and diamante collar and jumped and twisted as people laughed.

Sophie snorted.

"Buggles is better behaved than that."

"In second place is Lena with her pet, Marmaduke."

A girl and her mother walked up with a large fluffy ginger cat in a cage. The judges handed her a blue rosette.

Sophie wrinkled her nose.

"In first place –" the man with the microphone waited a moment, letting the tension hang in the air. "In first place is Philip with his pet, Ratty."

There was a huge round of applause as Philip went up to claim his prize, a white rat perched on his shoulder. He was handed a red rosette and a cup big enough to hold a boiled egg. He punched the air with his fist and grinned widely.

"A rat! How can you love a rat?" Sophie asked. When Fiona looked down she saw Sophie's eyes were watery.

It was a quiet walk home and Fiona shot Sophie worried looks. As soon as the front door opened Sophie ran upstairs and flung herself on her bed. Fiona stared after her.

"I'll go," Kieran said quietly. "Ring me?"

Fiona nodded.

"I'm sorry. It's just that it's difficult for her at present. For so long, it was just the two of us."

Kieran gave her a kiss and let himself out of the front door. Fiona went upstairs and sat on the edge of Sophie's bed. She put a hand on her daughter's shoulder. Sophie was sobbing, her whole body shaking.

"Why didn't he win, Mum?"

"Oh, Sophie. Not everyone could win. There were lots of pets there."

"But Buggles is the best!"

"People see things in different ways. What's lovely to one person isn't always to someone else."

Fiona sat with her, stroking her head and back. Gradually the tears subsided and Sophie sat up and snuggled into Fiona's arms.

"Sophie, why don't you like Kieran? Has he ever done anything or said anything to make you unhappy?"

While they'd been sitting there Buggles had sneaked upstairs and wriggled himself on to the bed. She looked back at Sophie for an answer.

"He's big and hairy."

Fiona rocked back in surprise. She thought about it. Kieran was tall, over six feet, and broad. He worked outside on building sites. He did have thick wavy hair, a hairy chest and dark hair on his arms, but it had never bothered her.

"That doesn't matter, Sophie." Fiona laughed. "It's what's inside that counts, not how people look. Like the pets at the show. Ratty isn't beautiful, but he's a great pet. Did you see the way he sat on Philip's shoulder?"

Sophie nodded and had the grace to blush, a red stain travelling up her neck to her face.

"Do you think you could attempt to be nice? Kieran is trying very hard to get to know you. And," Fiona added, "I like him very much."

Sophie nodded again.

"OK. He's offered to take us to the beach tomorrow. I'd really like to go, if you would."

"The beach? Oh, yes!" Sophie looked up, her eyes gleaming.

*     *     *     *

They had a great day by the sea. With his building expertise, Kieran helped Sophie build an impressive sandcastle with a moat and towers.

Sophie asked him lots of questions about his job and seemed genuinely intrigued by the answers. A new world was slowly opening up to her.

Later, they paddled in the sea — Fiona declared it too cold to swim — and Buggles chased seagulls on the dunes afterwards. Before they drove home they bought fish and chips and sat in Kieran's car to eat them.

Sophie behaved impeccably and Fiona was proud of her.

"Bath and bed," she said when they got home.

"Shall I read you a story, Sophie?" Kieran offered.

Fiona's eyes widened. That might be pushing the relationship too far, but Sophie appeared happy with the offer.

## Stranger At The Inn

Every year folk pause to see,
To look, and to admire,
Our church's own nativity –
A scene meant to inspire!
Carved in wood, and decades old,
A treasure that we all behold.

But this year, what had come to pass?
For with the Holy Family,
Angels and shepherds, ox and ass,
Something we didn't think to see,
For in the manger, nestling there
Was a little teddy bear!

We soon found out who was to blame,
A little voice piped up to say,
"I thought it was a dreadful shame,
For Baby Jesus, night and day,
To have no toys tucked up in bed.
And so I thought he could have Ted!"

And you know what? After a while,
I swear I saw the baby smile!

**Deborah Mercer.**

"OK. I choose."

Fiona listened to what was going on in Sophie's room as she tidied the bathroom.

"Which story, then?"

"My family story."

"Really? This one? It's broken. Are all the pages here?"

"It's all there." Sophie's voice was prim. "And it's a great story. It doesn't matter what the book looks like. It's what inside that counts. That's what Mummy says."

Fiona heard Kieran clear his throat. He's probably trying not to laugh, she thought.

"You're a clever girl," she heard him say. "And I'll tell you something else. Mummies are always right." ■

# Wedding Gloves

## by Michelle J. Heatley

"YOU must *always* wear gloves at a party," Aunt Gloria said, her head buried in the bottom drawer of the solid pine chest. "In my day a lady would never dream of attending a dance without wearing a pair of elegant gloves."

It was May 1944 and Rene's seventeenth birthday was only a few days away. Rene's mother had been determined to push the boat out, to have a "really good do" for Rene's party, and had spent most of the week making the birthday cake, using powdered egg and a whole month's ration of sugar.

"Rene," she'd said, "you are going to have the best birthday party this street has ever seen. After all, there is no knowing what is around the corner."

Rene waited patiently while Aunt Gloria pulled the contents from the drawer: a lacy tablecloth, a set of pillowcases with forget-me-nots embroidered in each corner and six starched linen napkins.

"Here they are," she said triumphantly, holding up a glove box. For a moment, Aunt Gloria's fingers caressed the dark red velvet, and then, with a look of eagerness mixed with sadness, she lifted the lid. "These were for my wedding day. I never got to wear them."

Rene perched on the edge of Aunt Gloria's bed looking at the pair of gloves nestling on the silk lining. Everyone called her Rene and not Irene, but she quite liked it because she felt Rene didn't sound too old-fashioned.

Aunt Gloria had moved in with them after she was evacuated from her top-floor flat, in a block near the docks, when one of Hitler's bombs struck it.

She'd ignored the policeman blocking her way, telling him, "I've lived through one war and a bit of precarious masonry is not going to stop me, thank you very much!"

*Illustration by iStock.*

The indomitable aunt had persuaded the policeman to help her haul out a battered, but mostly intact, pine chest of drawers.

In her determined no-nonsense way, Aunt Gloria had decided that nothing else would do for Rene's special day. The gloves matched Rene's dress, which was made from her mother's ivory silk wedding dress, altered in the spirit of "make do and mend".

Rene didn't know what to say as she carefully picked up the gloves; they were the softest leather and exactly the right shade of old ivory. Without thinking, she slipped her hand into one of the gloves, feeling the leather on her fingers, like wearing a second skin.

"Thank you," Rene whispered, the glove reaching up to her elbow. "They are really lovely. Are you sure I can wear them?"

"I am absolutely sure. They've been in that drawer for too many years, along with all these things I'd collected for my wedding day," Aunt Gloria said as she folded the pillowcases, the lacy tablecloth and the linen napkins, putting them carefully back in the drawer.

"My Walter had been given a spot of leave. We'd even booked the church. I remember how excited I was when I heard the knock at the door and thought it was him." Aunt Gloria sighed and reached into her apron pocket, taking out a telegram, crumpled and edged in black.

"There are not enough words here to tell you that the man you love will not be coming home, are there?"

Rene looked at the gloves and couldn't imagine how awful Aunt Gloria must have felt on hearing the tragic news; she never got the chance to lay her head on the embroidered pillowcases with her beloved husband.

Aunt Gloria often took out the telegram, reading it slowly, but once she'd shed a tear she would slip it back into her apron pocket.

Rene knew that once Aunt Gloria had shaken off her sadness, she would be the life and soul of the party. She might have never married, but Aunt Gloria loved to have fun.

* * * *

At last, it was the day of Rene's party.

The church hall was decorated in swathes of patriotic bunting, and Rene thought it looked lovely, if a little bit too red, white and blue for a birthday.

Everyone had chipped in, using most of their weekly ration for the meat paste, egg and cheese sandwiches, arranged on a long trestle table.

In pride of place was the cake her mother had made. It stood three tiers high; the bottom two layers were made of decorated cardboard, and perched on the top was a feather-light sponge cake with home-made jam in the middle and a dusting of sugar on the top.

In the packed church hall, Uncle Reginald, who had lost a leg in the last war, played the piano. Rene spent the evening being twirled around the floor by a succession of uncles, friends of the family and friends of friends.

Eventually, exhausted and with aching feet, she slumped on to one of the wooden chairs at the edge of the hall.

After catching her breath, she noticed a young lad watching her. He was dressed in a khaki uniform a size too big, his hands disappearing up his sleeves. He sidled over to Rene, blushing redder than the bunting fluttering above their heads.

"C . . . can I have the n . . . next dance?" he stuttered.

Rene thought he looked like a little lost boy, but when he smiled she saw his eyes were the deepest chocolate brown, twinkling with fun.

"Yes, I would like that."

"Oh, great," he said, the words whooshing out as if relieved she'd said yes. "My name is Michael, but everyone calls me Mick."

"I'm Irene, but everyone calls me Rene," she said, holding out a gloved hand.

One dance became two dances, and in between Rene and Mick talked about what they wanted when the war ended.

All too soon, the night was over. When Mick turned to say goodbye, Rene asked him if they would see each other again.

"You look lovely in these gloves," he said, taking hold of her hand.
"I would really like to see you again, but we've all been recalled to base.
Will you wait for me?"

Unable to speak, Rene nodded, and knew she would wait for Mick no
matter how long it took.

Rene watched Aunt Gloria laughing at a joke told by Uncle Reginald,
and gripped Mick's hand. What if he never came home? She couldn't
bear to think about never seeing him again.

Six days after the party the radio announced that the troops had
landed in France. Rene wondered if Mick was over there, and when she
returned the gloves to Aunt Gloria she told her all about him.

*　*　*　*

"I can't get married without proper gloves, Nana Rene. My wedding
dress, my hat and the shoes are perfect, but . . ."

"I think I have just what you need, Betsy, dear," Rene said, smiling at
the young woman sitting on the end of her bed.

Rene opened the battered pine chest and from the drawer she
carefully took out the faded lace tablecloth, two pillowcases with pale
blue forget-me-nots embroidered in the corners, the cotton yellowed
with age, and the set of creased linen napkins.

"Here it is," Rene said, holding up a long, thin, red velvet box and
handing it to Betsy.

Though christened Elizabeth, everyone called her Betsy. Rene knew
she preferred the shorter version of her name, as it sounded more
old-fashioned. It made Rene laugh that, in this modern age, Betsy
wanted to live in the past.

In five days' time, Betsy would be marrying the love of her life, Andy.
The village hall had been booked. Betsy had found her perfect wedding
dress, made from parachute silk and decorated with antique lace and
pearls, in a vintage shop.

When Betsy told her about it Rene had laughed – in her day they were
called second-hand shops. The hat with birdcage veil was Betsy's
mother's – not quite wartime chic, but it looked beautiful all the same.

Betsy had said she didn't want to be a frothy white bride, the sort the
wedding magazines show floating down the aisle in French lace and
gossamer.

"Here you are." Rene handed Betsy the familiar box. "These gloves
were given to me by my aunt Gloria to wear at my birthday party."

"How lovely!" Betsy gasped, staring at the ivory elbow-length soft
leather gloves. "They're just what I've been looking for."

"Tell me how you met Andy again," Rene urged, knowing she never got
tired of listening to the story.

Betsy snuggled next to Rene and told her the story of how she and
Andy met at a VE Day dance, celebrating the 70th anniversary of the
end of the war.

She then handed Rene a photograph of a young man dressed in
soldier attire, all khaki and shiny buttons.

He reminds me so much of when I first met my Mick, Rene mused.

"Andy loves this period; he says it was exciting as people lived life as if there were no tomorrow."

Rene busied herself putting away the napkins, but couldn't tell the younger woman how it really was. Exciting, maybe, but mainly it was frightening not knowing if your loved ones would ever return home, like Aunt Gloria's Walter.

"When he asked me to marry him," Betsy continued, "I remember thinking it might be fun, dressing up as someone from the past." She giggled. "I'm so excited, Nana Rene."

When Betsy was young, she'd lived next door to Rene, who wasn't her real nana. She'd help her make cakes and Rene would tell her about the war and how she used powdered egg, while Betsy licked the spoon.

She would listen for hours to Rene's stories, about life during the war, of hiding under the stairs when the bombing got too close.

She would clap her hands with delight when Rene described her seventeenth birthday party and how she first met her Mick.

"He was so handsome and painfully shy," Rene had often said.

\*　\*　\*　\*

Betsy's wedding day was perfect. The village hall, decorated with red, white and blue bunting, reminded Rene of her birthday party all those years ago.

Betsy's ivory parachute silk dress skimmed her hips, and she looked lovely in matching shoes and the hat with birdcage veil. But best of all, she was wearing Aunt Gloria's skin-soft wedding gloves.

When Andy led Betsy into the centre of the floor, he lifted up her gloved hand and kissed it, accompanied by a young man bashing out "We'll Meet Again" on the piano. Andy whirled Betsy around the floor, much to everyone's delight.

Rene's mind became a mixture of emotions, both past and present.

"They look so happy," a voice said next to Rene.

Rene turned her head and Mick's chocolate-brown eyes stared into hers. Rene reached across the table and entwined her hands into his.

"Just like we were on our wedding day, Mick, darling."

"Just like we are now," he added.

"Betsy asked me if I wore the gloves on our wedding day," Rene said, squeezing his fingers.

"What did you say?"

"That it was not a glove and hat wedding," Rene replied, smiling. "I told her we married in the local registry office as St Stephen's church spire had been damaged when one of those Buzz Bombs landed.

"And I told her something which I know Aunt Gloria would have approved of – that the wedding gloves have been waiting for the one special day they could be worn."

Later, as Rene and Mick watched Andy and Betsy dance around the floor, bunting fluttering above their heads, it was just like stepping back in time. ▪

**F**RANK CAPRA'S Christmas classic has been enchanting audiences for decades. But the festive favourite was almost a box-office flop, opening to mixed reviews and failing to make enough money on initial release to cover the costs of making it.

It tells the story of George Bailey (James Stewart) who, deeply in debt and feeling he's let everyone down, wishes he'd never been born. Having been tricked by the town's unscrupulous and greedy slum landlord, Henry Potter, George's Buildings & Loan company is bust and there's a warrant out for his arrest. As George contemplates ending his life on a snowy Christmas Eve, his guardian angel Clarence (Henry Travers) intervenes. He shows him an alternative Bedford Falls, one where George had never existed. It's not a pretty picture. George ultimately realises how much value his life has had for his loved ones, his community and even the wider world.

"Remember, George, no man is a failure who has friends," Clarence tells his charge.

The uplifting message of the film captured the hearts of everyone who saw it. It remained Frank Capra's favourite film of all those he directed, and is now considered one of the greatest films of all time.

# Whatever The Weather

## by Valerie Bowes

E'D been looking forward to this for weeks. Weeks when the weather had been as warm and sunny as you could expect in summer. When it didn't matter. And now look at it! George traced, with a disconsolate finger, the descent of a raindrop on the windowpane.

"Will it clear up?" he asked.

Seeing the flat, grey, sullen look of the clouds, even his ten-year-old's optimism couldn't make himself believe it would.

His mum came to slip an arm around his shoulders.

"Remember what Gran always says? Whether the weather be fine . . ."

George wriggled free. He didn't want to hear it. Not again. It was the silliest poem he'd ever heard. And he definitely didn't want to hear it today.

"Yes, well, I don't like it," he said, trying not to shout or he'd be told off for being rude. As if being sent to his room could make this day any worse.

"It's the Sunday school trip, Mum. We were going on the train to the seaside. Why did it have to rain today? They'll call it off, won't they?"

"Let's go down to the station and see if anyone else is there," she suggested. "We can always come back if everybody's decided that it's just too wet. But you never know, it might fair up by the time we get to Weston."

Looking up at the solidly sunless sky, George didn't think so, but he bundled on his mac and his cap and his stoutest shoes, pulling his socks up neatly.

Mum packed his sandwiches and a slice of cake into a bag and they squelched their way along the street, huddled together under an umbrella.

The spokes were slightly bent on one side, so that water dripped down the back of George's neck. It seemed to sum up the day.

But when they reached the station, the porter waved them past with a grin.

"Sunday school party? Straight through, then, madam. Have a good time, young fellow-me-lad."

Everyone was waiting on the platform. Ronnie Jones and Basil Stansfield waved at him as he detached himself from his mother's side and raced to join them in watching eagerly down the shining rails for the first sign of the locomotive.

"There it is!" Ronnie pointed, his freckled face shining with anticipation, his hair dripping down his nose.

They jiggled up and down as the funnel pushed grey puffs into the air like smoke-signals, half wanting to run back to the crowd of mothers and children but entranced by the sight of the engine, the scarlet board across the front gleaming with rain.

"Get the number?" Ronnie asked excitedly.

George didn't have his notebook with him, but Basil nodded. He never went anywhere without it.

The sky showed no sign of lightening, but the excitement as they all piled into the carriages couldn't have been greater.

And then, with a great gush of steam and a chuff-chuff-chuff as the wheels got a grip, they were off.

George couldn't really remember it raining at the seaside, but the beach was yellow instead of pale, like Biscuit the retriever's coat, and there were puddles all along the prom.

The boys got told off for jumping in them and splashing the girls, but no-one really cared.

Ruby Marsh didn't even squeal when the spray went all over her white socks.

People from the local church came to meet them and take them to their hall. One beefy chap, with a jolly red face like a beardless Father Christmas and a voice like a fog-horn, soon had them playing Man The Lifeboat.

After all the rushing about, Port to Starboard, Fore to Aft, snapping to attention for Captain's Coming, diving flat for Bombs Coming Over, and balancing in wobbly laughter at Freeze!, they were glad to sit down and share out the food they'd brought with them.

The people from the church had brought extra cakes and there were even great plates of jelly, blocks of strawberry and vanilla ice-cream and glasses of lemon and orangeade.

Some of the ladies manned the great urn which steamed as richly as the locomotive and provided tea for the grown-ups. Then they played some more games until it was time to catch the train home.

We never missed the sea and the beach, George realised as he thought about it. All the other times they'd gone to the seaside blurred into one sunshiny day, but the Wet Sunday School Trip was the one everyone remembered.

Ruby had always teased him about jumping in that puddle.

\* \* \* \*

It had been snowing that Saturday. Snowing on top of roads wet with the icy drizzle that had preceeded it. A recipe for disaster.

Ruby told him he was worrying too much about it when the pains started. It was a false alarm, that was all. The baby wasn't due for another couple of weeks at least.

"Everything all right, love?"

"Fine," she said, massaging her swollen stomach. "Must have given an extra hard kick, I reckon."

"Ah, he's going to be a footballer, my lad. Another Geoff Hurst, you mark my words. Want a cup of tea?"

"No, thanks. I feel a bit queasy."

"You just sit back and put your feet up, then."

It had only been about half an hour later that he heard her groan. Panic flooded his chest and threatened to spill out of his mouth, but George had to keep himself together.

He wasn't any use to her if he was a quivering heap of indecision.

He paused in the hall outside the sitting-room to take a deep, steadying breath, then pushed open the door with an assumption of nonchalance.

"You OK?"

She shook her head, blowing her breath out in small gusts.

"We'd better call the midwife, then," he said, trying to sound as if it was something they did every day. Nothing special.

Ruby gestured at the window. Outside in the steel-grey afternoon, snow was whirling on a flirty breeze. The hedges bore shawls of white and the roofs were doing their best to look like the Christmas cards that had been taken down only ten days ago.

"Think she'll be able to get here? She's got to come from over the other side of town."

"I'll give her a ring."

It would choose today, he thought, dialling the number and not entirely sure whether he meant the snow or the baby. He could cope with either on its own.

Whether he could cope with the combination of the two was another matter. But he had to. There was no choice.

Out of the blue, his grandmother's little verse popped into his head. *Whether the weather be fine, or whether the weather be not . . .*

Maybe, but Gran hadn't had to cope with a baby which was on the way and a midwife who probably wasn't. He rang anyway, but the lady on the other end could give him no comfort.

"I'm awfully sorry. She went out on another case and she should have been back by now. It's this wretched snow, you know."

"I just hope she hasn't had an accident. Or got stuck in a snowdrift. Someone told me it's quite bad out Twiston way."

It was bad enough him being worried sick. He didn't want to add to her burden.

"It'll just be the traffic, I expect. Crawling along. Tell her not to worry. I'll take my wife to the hospital so she's not to try to get over here."

That's burned my boats now, he thought, putting the phone back and reaching for the car keys. Nothing for it but to get Ruby there as quickly as possible, but driving through the town, he'd never been so scared.

The roads were more like the slides they'd made in the playground as kids. All his instincts were to push his foot down on the pedal as far as he could, but he couldn't.

He had to creep along, listening to Ruby trying not to let the yells of pain escape her.

"Hold on, love," George encouraged her, wondering what on earth he'd do if they didn't make it in time.

It was all very well, these stories you heard about babies being delivered by the side of the road, but he wouldn't know where to start. And what about poor Ruby?

He saw the entrance of the hospital with a thankfulness that washed from his chilled toes to his head.

"It's all right, love. We're here," he said, and moved his foot to the brake.

But his shoe got tangled in his flares, he pushed harder than he intended, and the car turned sideways and glided gracefully into the stone pillar on Ruby's side of the car with a gentle bump.

\* \* \* \*

"You were born, there on the front seat," he told his daughter when she was a teenager. "I couldn't shift the car for your mum to get out.

"The wheels just spun and I was afraid of doing more damage and bringing the pillar down on top of us."

"Oh, Dad! What a nightmare! What did you do? Deliver me yourself?"

"No. I didn't want to leave your mum, so I just yelled for help until the nurses came running, but by then, you were on the way."

"I'll bet if I'd been a boy you'd have called me Ford." Jackie laughed. "Still, all's well that ends well, eh, Dad?"

He never let on, especially to Susan and David, but somehow Jackie was the most precious to him of all their children.

It wasn't because she was their first. It was because of how it might have all gone so wrong.

He couldn't remember what the weather was like when her younger sister and brother were born, but he'd always remember that snowstorm.

*   *   *   *

He knew Jackie and Susan had made a magnificent cake, decorated with gold ribbons and gilded candles, with 50 in big gold letters.

David had been lovingly marinading chops and chicken for hours in delicious-looking sauces with carefully chopped herbs and spices blended as only he knew how, and there were plastic boxes holding different salads lurking in the garage under an innocently draped tablecloth.

George and Ruby weren't supposed to know anything about it. But they did. Of course they did, but they wouldn't spoil the surprise.

And it was the perfect day for a barbecue that everyone had been praying for. Except George and Ruby.

*Whether the weather be fine, or whether the weather be not.*
*Whether the weather be cold or whether the weather be hot,*
*We must weather the weather, whatever the weather,*
*Whether we like it or not.*

They'd had the lot, over the last 60-odd years. The wet Sunday school trip; the snow and the anxiety when Jackie was born; the thunderstorm that put the power out of action one Christmas so they had to make do without televison and have their turkey on Boxing Day – the best Christmas they'd ever had, everybody reckoned; the hurricane that meant all the neighbours pooling petrol-driven power-saws and clearing up the trees that had fallen across their gardens.

A right community spirit blossoming out of disaster, that had been. Ruby and the other women had dug out camping equipment and somehow kept them all supplied with mugs of tea and sandwiches.

These things stayed with you longer by far than the nice days when everything went smoothly.

Which was why, although they couldn't do anything about the weather, he and Ruby had a few surprises of their own planned for this party.

It was a good job it was forecast to be one of the hottest days of the year, because the garden hose snaking around the flower-beds was suddenly going to be springing an awful lot of holes . . . ■

# Anstruther, Fife

Known locally as Anster, this bustling fishing village attracts many tourists keen to sample the local award-winning fish and chips – the fish is so fresh, they even name the boat the catch came in on!

Anstruther is the largest of the fishing villages dotted along the East Neuk of Fife. Enjoy visiting the array of gift and craft shops as you watch the hustle and bustle of harbour life, or explore the abundance of rock pools.

It's part of the Fife coastal path, and walkers will love exploring the neighbouring villages, too. Or you can take one of the regular pleasure boat trips out to the Isle of May which run regularly from April through to September.

Along with a variety of birds, the isle is home to the puffin and there are magical tales of Vikings and smugglers, too.

With wynds to unwind in, the stresses of everyday life will melt away as you tread the cobbled streets built on a rich fishing history.

# A Change At Christmas

## by Lucy Chester

O N a rainy, late November day, Rachel was looking, without enthusiasm, at a Christmas cake recipe, when her phone rang. She picked it up.

"No! I'm so sorry to hear that!" She looked up at Jack, who was fitting light bulbs in the kitchen ceiling.

"Aunt Mary's broken her ankle. She can't come for Christmas."

"It'll just be us and the kids then," Jack said.

For years now, from when the children had been small, to now in their teenage years, Rachel's aunt Mary had come up from the West Country to join them for Christmas.

Every year Rachel painted a picture of kindness and charity to her friends – Aunt Mary has no children of her own, she's widowed and lives alone, so she comes to join us for a proper family Christmas.

But the truth was, they needed Mary quite as much as she needed them. Her arrival always meant a welcome change of atmosphere in the house.

Both Rachel's parents had passed away, and she was an only child, so Mary was her only close relative. Jack had no-one nearby, either.

Mary was a sparky character, great at introducing new card games to the children, working out the rules of board games and making them fun, while Rachel and Jack prepared the feast.

And the children were growing up now. Amy, the eldest, was fourteen, her sister Beth just one year younger, and their brother Craig, ten.

Rachel sighed at the thought of going through all the rituals of Christmas again without the support of Aunt Mary, and also now without the support of her daughters.

Teenager Amy was beginning to kick back a bit against family.

"I'm rather afraid Amy will open presents, stay for Christmas lunch then rush straight off to see her friend Kamryn," Rachel said. "And Beth will want to go with her, so there'll just be Craig left here wanting to play computer games." She bent to get the mixing bowl from the cupboard.

Illustration by iStock.

"Kamryn. I feel she's not a good influence, but there's nothing I can really pin down about her. Amy was doing well at school – but not lately."

"Kamryn is very grown up for her age," Jack observed, "and our girls admire that. Also, she's left alone too much. They admire that, too."

The next day a letter arrived from Aunt Mary.

*Dear Rachel and Jack,*

*Wi-Fi is a bit iffy in my house and I can't get up to the community centre to e-mail you, so I'm writing the old way.*

*I've a suggestion. Some neighbours here visit their daughter in Scotland for a month every Christmas. I've spoken to them – their house is empty, so why don't you come down here, for a change?*

*As you know I live right on the edge of Dartmoor. Plenty of places for you all to go walking and exploring.*

"Let's go," Jack said promptly, when Rachel showed him the letter that evening. "In fact, let's go for the whole holiday period."

"No way!" Amy exclaimed. "I had plans for Christmas Day evening and Boxing Day with Kamryn. And I bet there's no signal down there."

"It'll be something different," Rachel said, "and we can't leave poor Aunt Mary on her own."

Amy sighed heavily.

"Sounds boring." Then she brightened up. "Can't I stay here?"

Jack had been checking his phone.

"You know Mary lives on the edge of Dartmoor," he said.

Amy groaned.

"You're not going to suggest hiking!"

"Not if you don't want to," Jack said. "But there are wild ponies living on Dartmoor. Lots of them."

At this, Rachel, watching Amy, saw a quick gleam of interest in her face.

"There are lots of myths and legends around Dartmoor. One is that there is a large pack of black hounds that roam the moors at night.

"Another is that on a night of the full moon, in a place not far from where your great-aunt lives, an army of Roman Legionaries has been seen."

Beth and Craig moved up closer to him as he spoke.

"Also, there is the Crazywell Pool, said to be bottomless. Look into it and you will see the next person who will die."

The children gasped. Jack gave a hint of a wink to Rachel over their heads.

\* \* \* \*

The car journey to Aunt Mary's was long and tedious, with the children sulky and quarrelsome.

Rachel got out of the car with relief. She greeted her aunt effusively, to mask the surly expressions of her two daughters.

Mary, bright-eyed as ever, sat beside her blazing wood-burning stove, with one leg propped on a stool, a yellow Labrador sprawled at her feet. The room was cosy, with squashy armchairs.

"This is Margaret," Mary indicated another lady about the same age as herself, "who is spending the day with me. Come in and have some tea."

Rachel went with Margaret into the kitchen to help with the tea-making.

When they emerged with a trayful of mugs, Amy was sitting on the rug stroking the Labrador's head, which he acknowledged with a thumping tail.

"When you've settled into the house up the street," Mary said, twinkling up at Rachel as she held out the keys, "Amy and Beth are going to come and take poor Marley out for his walk before it gets dark.

"He's getting on, but he likes his exercise three times a day. It's been hard for him with me like this."

The house they were to stay in was old but restored. Apart from books on the shelves and paintings on the walls, it was bare of all family clutter.

The bareness was balm to Rachel's soul, and her spirits lifted. As in Mary's house, there was a wood-burning stove.

"Always wanted one of these," Jack said. Their own small modern house had no fireplace. "There's a pile of logs outside. Let's get it going. Coming, Craig?"

Rachel saw that Amy and Beth had dumped their bags in their room and gone straight back to Mary's.

Pleased they'd found an activity so quickly, Rachel hummed in the kitchen as she unpacked the food she'd brought.

Already, in the garden, Jack and Craig had piled chopped logs in the wheelbarrow, and were digging up the Christmas tree.

Amy and Beth came in presently, flushed and exhilarated from walking Marley.

"Cold out there!" Amy cried happily. "Marley is such an obedient dog. Knows where he's going, and always comes when he's called."

On Christmas Eve they decorated the tree with a few things Rachel had brought down with her, plus some holly with red berries, trailing leaves of varied shades of green. Beth made a line of paper dolls.

"Different from our usual," Rachel said, enjoying the odd-looking tree.

"We're going to church tonight," she announced later.

"I'll stay here," Amy said.

"And me," Beth added quickly.

Rachel took a deep breath.

"Aunt Mary can't walk up the hill at the moment, so she's asked if you two would push her chair."

"Oh, OK, then."

\* \* \* \*

"Hate this thing," Mary said, cheerfully tapping her wheelchair as the girls pushed her up the road. "But aren't I lucky it's just for a few weeks?"

The church was beautiful. Its ancient nave was lit by circular branches of candles that hung from the high arched ceiling.

The candlelight gave a lustre to the stained-glass windows, and threw shadows on to the nativity scene. A choir with many young members stood at the back of the church. Their faces were earnest as they processed up the aisle, their pure voices breaking into harmony and soaring over the top notes.

Beth was entranced.

"I think I might join the school choir," she whispered to Rachel.

Afterwards, over mulled wine and mince-pies, Mary introduced Rachel and her family to her numerous friends. She seemed to know the whole congregation.

Rachel saw Beth talking brightly to a girl with blue stripes in her hair, who'd sung a thrilling solo,

That evening on her way to bed, Rachel stopped briefly outside the girls' room.

"Wonder how Kamryn is? I've sent texts but she hasn't replied. Rubbish signal down here," she heard Amy say. "We were going to do something on Christmas afternoon, hang out round the park or shops." She yawned. "I'd better get to sleep; got to get up early to walk Marley."

Rachel smiled and moved away.

On Christmas morning, as the turkey sizzled and spat in the oven, Rachel stood at the sink, scraping carrots and parsnips. Amy was out with Marley. Mary sat with Beth at the kitchen table, peeling sprouts.

"We spent a whole science lesson once dissecting a sprout," Beth said.

"No," Mary said. "Not a whole lesson!"

Beth giggled.

"Shall I show you? There's a lot to a sprout, you know."

Jack and Craig had been out in the garden gathering logs again. Now they came in, boosted the fire and started laying the table.

In the course of the morning, four of Mary's friends dropped in to say happy Christmas. Never, Rachel thought, have we had so many visitors on a Christmas morning.

The friends came with gifts. A bottle of ginger beer, a jar of jam, a plant, a small knitted dog.

"Where's Marley and Amy?" Mary said.

Just then girl and dog surged in together through the back door. Rachel saw that Amy's face was radiant. She looked years younger, an uncomplicated child again.

Marley went straight through to the sitting-room and flopped down in front of the fire. Mary laughed.

"You've worn my poor old boy out."

Christmas lunch went well at the big dining table, and afterwards they all sat round the fire.

"Charades?" Rachel suggested.

Amy made retching sounds.

"This house is very old," Mary said, ignoring her. "Built long before television was invented. People at Christmas time used to play games together, and sing round the piano, so we'll honour the old place and do some charades. Did you know your mum once wanted to be an actress?"

"It's true, so I did!" Rachel exclaimed. "I'd almost forgotten. But my job means a steady income, which we need."

Over the following days, with the promise of seeing wild ponies, Rachel and Jack took their family on to Dartmoor.

They dressed warmly, and explored the rough grey-green expanses of the moor with its jagged clumps of rock. They found the ponies in small groups, often in sheltered places.

On their last day in Devon they set off early.

"I'm feeling fitter from all this hiking already," Jack said, and the children made no complaint as they pulled on their boots.

The weather had turned icy cold, and a freezing wind with flakes of snow blew in their faces. They walked quickly, up a hill and deep into the moor. They stopped for a short rest by a pond that was partially iced over.

Craig crouched down to inspect pieces of ice, like panes of glass, that had broken off and lay around the edges of the pond.

He picked up the glossy pieces and sent them skimming over the thin ice surface, then watched them shatter and slide into the water at the back. Amy and Beth joined in his game, picking up pieces of ice in their gloved hands.

Rachel looked around her. The moor, hills and tors spread out as far as the eye could see. There was no house, no human in sight.

Suddenly a drumming began in the earth under their feet, turning into a dull rhythmic thudding. Craig and Beth pressed up against Jack, and

Amy drew nearer to him.

Then she screamed out as a herd of ponies stampeded over the moor towards them. Bay ponies, strong and free, with sturdy bodies and rough, wild-flowing manes and tails.

After a few seconds, another group galloped past.

The children had stopped crying out, and watched in wonder. Amy moved across the track to see how many more ponies were joining the stampede.

Through a sudden thick flurry of snow, a final group of ponies cantered past in the direction of the rest of the herd.

"Where's Amy?" Jack asked sharply.

The snow blocked their vision, and the light was now fading fast. They called out, but the freezing wind whipped their voices back at them.

After some minutes of shouting and panicking, the snowfall stopped. Through a clear gap they saw a glimpse of a yellow scarf waving.

"I thought I'd really lost you!" Amy said tearfully, holding tight to Jack's arm. But after a short while, she recovered.

"You know that last group of ponies, the straggly older ones? It was like they saw me on my own and slowed right down. It was amazing!"

"I've read," Jack said, "that if there are injured ponies in the herd, some of them will stop and move at the pace of the slowest member, to give them time. Maybe they did that with you."

"You know, Mum," Amy said, when they were nearly back at the house, "animals are magic. I think I want to be a vet."

\*　\*　\*　\*

"Mary, thank you so much!" Rachel hugged her aunt as they said goodbye the following day. "Really, you've put us all back on track."

"Nonsense, dear, you're doing just fine," Mary said bracingly. "Come back next year!"

Rachel drove for the first part of the journey home. There was an air of content in the car, so different from the fractious drive down.

In the passenger seat, Jack was looking at his phone.

"I'm looking at hill-walking groups."

Rachel also began to weave plans of her own. There was a dance and drama academy in their town. Maybe she could do an evening class?

"We don't really have to feel sorry for Great-aunt Mary, do we?" Amy said.

"No, we don't!" Rachel laughed. "She's a complete inspiration."

"You know, Amy, if Kamryn is on her own quite a bit, maybe she'd like to come over to ours to do homework with you? One more to cook for is no problem."

To her surprise Amy nodded.

"Good idea. Thanks, Mum."

Rachel smiled. A new and welcome lightness of spirit had come to her during this Christmas break. The future seemed somehow more positive and hopeful for each of these, her most beloved people.

She pulled out confidently on to the motorway. ■

# The Pineapple, Airth

Known as Scotland's "most bizarre building", the Dunmore Pineapple at Airth, Stirlingshire, has an eye-catching, exotic look.

Built back in 1761 after being commissioned by the 4th Earl of Dunmore, John Murray, the folly served as a summerhouse complete with walled garden.

The building is perhaps a nod to the exotic fruits that were grown in the glasshouses here, in an era when pineapples represented a form of wealth and power. Only the well-off could afford to have the fruit grace their dinner tables when trying to impress guests.

The folly, set in woodland, is around 46 feet in height and is a great example of the work of the talented stonemasons of the day.

Just a short drive away you can see an entirely different structure on a massive scale – the Kelpies. These horse head structures are 30 metres high and were the creation of sculptor Andy Scott.

Also attracting tourists to the area is the Falkirk Wheel, an impressive rotating boat lift.